MICHAEL CORNELL

UNDER FRIENDLY FIRE

Edited by James Van Treese
Cover Art by R. M. Laslow

Northwest Publishing Inc.
5949 South 350 West
Salt Lake City, UT 84107
801-266-5900

Northwest Publishing Inc.
5949 South 350 West
Salt Lake City, Utah 84107
801-266-5900

Copyright 1993
by
Francis Michael Dattilo, Jr.

Typeset by
Accurate Word Processing Service
Dearborn, MI

ISBN #1-56901-059-5

Printed in the United States of America

To

James Byron Dean
of
Fairmount, Indiana

whose voice
from another era
signaled the
inspiration
for this book.

UNDER
FRIENDLY FIRE

Chapter 1

Dexter

UNDER FRIENDLY FIRE

ONE

Welcome to Dexter

The Friendliest City in the U.S.A.
Population: 21,714

Hometown of Desert Storm Hero
Lance Corporal Zachary Taylor McLachin

"We'll Miss You, Zed!"

    There must have been a thousand towns like this one between home and here, Riskin thought, only they did not have signs with background notes for the casual tourist of one-hundred words or more duration. And none of their billboards read "We'll Miss You, Zed!" What felt like the balled fist of a steel gauntlet drove up through Riskin's insides when he saw the words. He tried to define the source of the thrust and the best he could arrive at was an uneasy mixture of fear and conscience. The combination was potent enough to make him pull the old Jeep over to the gravel shoulder that flanked the two-laner into Dexter.

MICHAEL CORNELL

After what he had been through in the Gulf neither the ugly spectre of fear nor the dulling of qualms of conscience had any business accompanying him here.

What had happened had happened. He had squeezed the trigger. He had *not* given the order. He had *not* flown the chopper.

And who the hell was Zachary McLachin anyway? Audie Murphy? Did this town think that their homegrown boy was the first American soldier to lose his life in some faraway place with a strange-sounding name? Did they think he was the first one to get it like he got it, from the same side he was fighting on?

Riskin threw the Jeep noisily into first and pulled off the shoulder. It was getting dark and he wanted to see the widow tonight, not tomorrow morning, so he could move on. What he had to say to her would not take more than a half hour, he figured. After all, what *was* there to say. The whole thing was unfortunate. He was sorry. No. He had to do better than that. Such a direct approach had the tone of trivializing the incident. It sounded as though he had just run over her cat. But then how else was he to put it? Something would occur, he finally concluded, as the road curved to the left and houses, buildings came into view in the distance. It was somehow encouraging to see something other than flat farm land, mile after stinking mile of it.

UNDER FRIENDLY FIRE

Maybe it would take less than a half hour. Maybe she would not want to talk to him at all. Nothing personal, she might say, but you just killed my husband, that's all, so get the hell out of my face.

The small business district looked inviting, a welcome respite from the large, dirty cities he had grown up near. Near because his father's career as an Army lifer never had the family staying in one place for too long and always on a base just outside a metropolis of one size or another: large and larger. Dexter was different, something out of a corny sitcom rerun from the sixties. Small shops, diners, mom-and-pop stores. Not more than two of any variety. And *no* chains. It was remarkable to Riskin that such a town as Dexter still existed on the map or anywhere in America.

The sight of a small sliver of a barber shop with a light still on and the peppermint pole still revolving made him instinctively go to his chin, rub the one-day stubble. It made him feel dirty, unkempt. The feeling was a recurring one since his time in the Arab deserts. Upon his return stateside, he had shaved twice a day, showered as many as three times daily. It now seemed like days since he had shaved and showered early this morning before starting out on his trip. He pulled the Jeep into the diagonal parking slot directly in front of the barber shop.

MICHAEL CORNELL

The door was open. A wiry man in his late fifties, early sixties with a slight hunch sat in the third of three barber chairs watching a baseball game on a television set on a high shelf in the far corner of the room. The tv's audio was so low it might as well not been on. It did not seem to matter to the man in the chair who seemed to be in a trance, half-awake, half somewhere else. He still wore his blue half-smock but his shoes were neatly parked next to the old-time footrest that held his red-wool-stockinged feet.

"We're closed," he said quietly, matter-of-factly without ever seeming to look toward the door.

"Now that's some greeting for a returning soldier." Riskin shot back reflexively, then wondered why he had been such a smart-ass about it. "Then you mind if I give myself a shave?"

The man was already out of the chair and headed his way, shoeless, with an energy that Riskin would not have guessed possible.

"No self-serve around here," the man cracked amiably, "*especially* not for returning war heroes."

Now Riskin was really sorry, but he plopped his weary form into the first chair anyway.

"We had one from around here, we did," the man said as he threw a clean sheath over Riskin and fastened it behind the neck.

"One what?" Riskin asked although he already knew the answer.

UNDER FRIENDLY FIRE

"A war hero. A boy named McLachin."

"I saw the sign," Riskin returned with no inflection at all.

"How could you miss it? I told them it was too big. I sit in on the Chamber of Commerce meetings and I voiced my opinion," the man recounted with a certain fervor. "But I guessed they felt this kid deserved it."

"Why?" Riskin queried, feeling the resentment coming back.

"Circumstances, I suppose. His dad served two tours in Vietnam but that wasn't the half of it."

The man started laying the lather on Riskin's stubble, making him wait longer than he wanted for the other half.

"The main thing was Zed was a colorful kid around here, wild as all get-out but the best damned football player Dexter ever had and if there's one thing you should know about Dexter it's that it loves it's high school football. We got twenty-one-odd-thousand people here and the only ones who don't show up for the Friday night homegames is the ones on the Hill."

"I take it the Hill is the cemetery?"

"Serenity Hill. That's where the boy is buried. Somebody said he qualified for Arlington but all of Dexter wanted him back here. But then, the kid himself could've gone to Tennessee or Alabama on a football scholarship but he joined the Marines like his father. So detours were nothing new for Zed McLachin.

"Where'd he get a nickname like Zed?" Riskin asked, making small-talk as he felt the smooth strokes of the man's razor.

"The name of the high school team is the Zephyrs and somebody came up with the Zed. Literary obliteration I think you call it. But the funny thing is the Zephyrs. I looked it up once and the book said it was a gentle breeze. Well, there was nothing about Zed McLachin that answered to the description of a gentle breeze, far from it."

"What about his wife? What is she like?" Riskin was now distancing himself from the small talk.

"That's the other half of it," the man said, applying the final strokes before emitting a barely audible laugh. "That's funny: 'The other half of it.' That makes three halves, don't it?"

"I don't know. Does it?"

"Well, that fits McLachin, too. He only married the best looking girl Dexter's ever seen this side of a movie or a tv screen. The mayor's wife was a beauty queen once but Breezy McLachin makes her look like the lady-in-waiting."

"Breezy?" Riskin raised an eyebrow." As in 'zephyr'?"

UNDER FRIENDLY FIRE

"As in gentle breeze," the man chuckled with what seemed like irony, throwing a hot wet towel across Riskin's face. "Young thing but if you didn't notice, you're not male *or* female, women being the more jealous gender, wouldn't you say?"

"She still lives here, right?" Riskin asked without answering the question.

The man removed the towel just in time for Riskin to see the nod. "Say, you weren't in McLachin's company over there were you?"

"Nope. It may have been a short war but it was a big desert," came Riskin's reply. The smart-ass was returning too, and he wanted to check it.

"Sorry way to go though," was the man's nearly non-sequitur response. "Mowed down by your own side. Different if it was friendly Arabs."

Riskin wanted to get out of the chair right then but the man was poking him with a talcum brush, then sticking an oval mirror in his face. The reflection looked even older than the one this morning.

"Want me to trim the hedges some?" the man volunteered. "Those Army barbers are usually cooks who couldn't cut it in the messhall."

"I thought they were escaped psychos. Thanks anyway." Riskin climbed down from the chair, undoing the vinyl covering himself. "How much do I owe you?"

"You don't owe me nothing. Not after what you seen." The man started tidying things up with an almost military fastidiousness, the razor, the towel, the mirror. "I was just watching the ballgame anyway, being that I don't like going home nowadays."

"Troubles on the homefront, eh?"

"You might say that." The man was trying to sound nonchalant. "The missus ran off with this fella who was supposed to be an ordained minister. He wasn't from here, but Lord knows what he saw in her. She looks ten years older than she is. But I miss her just the same. But she'll be back. I hope so anyway."

Riskin felt sadder than the hunched barber sounded.

"Little town Dexter" the man said, "but it's gotta lot of those things they plant in the ground to explode when you walk on them."

"Land mines."

"Uh-huh."

Chapter 2

Zed

UNDER FRIENDLY FIRE

TWO

 The parallels between Zed McLachin and himself were not lost on Riskin. As he followed the barber's directions to the trailer court where the wife of a dead Marine lived, he reflected on the uncanny likenesses. McLachin was a star football player with scholarship offers from the likes of Tennessee and Alabama. Riskin was quite simply the best *white* high school basketball player to hail from his state in recent memory, with offers from a host of big schools who seemed undeterred by his relatively short six-foot stature. Like McLachin, he spurned the overtures and enlisted in the military. He had followed in the footsteps of his Army-lifer father as McLachin had followed the lead of *his* father, a career Marine--but not before sowing their respective share of proverbial wild oats. For Riskin, that had included several memorable run-ins with local law; from the barber's depiction of his unmet counterpart, McLachin had received few if any citizen citations himself. Too, both had served in Operation Desert Storm.

The parallel ended there.

There was something else. Not only had Riskin survived the war but he had left the service upon the expiration of his hitch, something it seemed unlikely for McLachin to do. And something he himself might not have done except for the incident. He had bought his freedom but from what he still was not certain. Leaving the restrictions of military life did not guarantee he had distanced himself from recollection of the regrettable occurrence. Blameless or not, it would stay with him awhile, probably longer.

The trailer park was poorly lit. Riskin almost drove past it, turning at the last moment. The dim, aging sign read "PROSPECT TRAILER PARK" but the site looked anything but. Ninety feet down the rutted, dirt drive, at the start of the trailers, he hit the brakes. Another much smaller sign said "Resident Managers: Luke and Lenora McLachin." Riskin wondered where the exclamation point was at the end of the names. Could this be Zed McLachin's parents? Resident managers of a trailer park seemed a suitable line of work for a retired Marine non-com--it wasn't likely Luke McLachin was an officer--and his wife. Without another moment's speculation, he turned the Jeep into the gravel path skirting the silver Airstream. A large ten-year-old Buick was parked under the faint

UNDER FRIENDLY FIRE

light coming from what must have been the trailer home's living room.

The door was already open when he walked up the path. A pretty, smallish woman around forty was waiting in the entrance way. Seeing her, Riskin was not sure if she were Zed McLachin's mother or his older sister. He chanced the first. It was difficult to believe the small trailer could have accommodated another family member.

"Mrs. McLachin?" He tried to sound as uncertain as he was.

"You're a friend of Zachary's," she said and opened the door as wide as it would open. "Luke, it's a friend of Zachary's," she announced over her shoulder before he could answer.

"Well, we were..." was all he could manage before trailing off at the sight of Mr. McLachin, a tall, solidly built man who looked to be a good fifteen years older than his wife.

"We were just talking about our son," the man greeted him, extending a large hand. "Come in, won't you."

Riskin shook the father's hand and was inside the tiny living room before the grip was loosed.

"Sit down," Mr. McLachin ordered him amicably, indicating the larger of two oversized chairs. "That's Zed's favorite when he drops by."

MICHAEL CORNELL

"I wish you would call him Zachary, dear," his wife corrected him.
"What's wrong with Zed? It's got color," the man argued.
"Anyway, our son likes Zed, he says so himself."
If the misplaced tense was bewildering, the room was downright disturbing to Riskin. The cramped living space was a veritable shrine to Zachary "Zed" McLachin. Athletic trophies of every size and metallic texture. And pictures. Zed in his football gear, his Marine dress-uniform, even his Desert Storm camous. In all of them he looked to be a young replica of his old man, tall, muscular, with a chip on his shoulder as big as Rushmore. The chip was not showing on the father right now. He was being very personable.
"How 'bout a Coke," he was saying. Before Riskin could decline, Mrs. McLachin had the ice-cold can in his hand. Now the pair stood over him in the chair as though he had come bearing news that would undo the terrible truth that had doubtlessly reached them months ago.
"You and Zed are pretty close, I bet," Luke McLachin continued without waiting for a response. His huge hands were knotted together as he hovered, spoke: "I bet you two are inseparable. In war, you gotta be. You get to know who your real friends are."
"What's your name?" the woman finally asked.

UNDER FRIENDLY FIRE

"Corporal James Riskin," he replied with a formality that even puzzled *him*. "Well, it *was* Corporal."

"You mean Lance Corporal, don't you, son?" the man interjected.

Riskin shook his head, "I was in the Army."

"But then how did Zed's *Marine* company get mixed in with yours?"

"Well, it was a pretty mixed up war, sir," he grinned awkwardly and took a quick gulp of the soft drink. It felt good going down.

"Zed was killed by an *Army* chopper," the big man suddenly stated. The tone, the way McLachin leaned forward, loomed over him in the chair made Riskin feel like the defendant in a bad courtroom drama. His testimony sustained the mood: "The Air Force had planes, the Navy had planes, and the Army had--"

"Choppers," the man interrupted him, then, inexplicably, seemed to soften. "Sorry, Corporal, I didn't mean to, well, you know, I didn't mean to..." he started without finishing.

"You have to realize it's very hard for us," his wife joined in.

Riskin seized the moment: "It's all right," he said getting up, "I understand how you feel, but I've got to be getting on tonight and I wanted to visit Zed's-- Zachary's widow."

MICHAEL CORNELL

"Did--Did you know Breezy?" Mrs. McLachin asked curiously. "I mean *before?*"

"This is the first time I've been in Dexter," Riskin answered.

"She wasn't from here," the woman said, still looking at him strangely.

"It's a big country," he returned.

"Are you being smart, boy?" the big man broke in.

"If I was smart--" I wouldn't have joined the Army, he stopped short without saying it. "No I'm not being smart," he said instead, handing the woman the still half-full Coke. "Now if you can tell me where to find Zed's wife--"

"She's probably not in her trailer," the woman informed him, "but you can try anyway."

She gave Riskin the directions. He left without saying goodbye to either of them.

He had been inside for only a matter of minutes but the night air seemed muggier, almost oppressive as he made his way back to the Jeep. Maybe it was not hotter at all, he reasoned. Maybe it had to do with his failed mission with the dead soldier's parents. He was *not* a friend of Zed McLachin. He had never even met the guy, had only encountered him once and that had been a deadly encounter at that. Sure, *they* had fabricated the friendship thing, but he did not have to string it along with his chicken-ass silence.

UNDER FRIENDLY FIRE

Riskin pushed the Jeep hard through the winding gravel lane to the back of the trailer park. Its short, choppy curves became a slalom course under the vehicle's wheels. A short, older man with a beer belly bursting from under his t-shirt started to cross, lunged back and cursed him at one turn.

With the widow it had to be different, he resolved. With her he must be open, direct, everything he was not with the McLachins. Your husband Zed--or did you call him Zachary?--was part of the Marine company on the ground. I was in one of the Apaches-- that's an Army attack copter, he would explain. It was night, desert night, the sand was blowing, obscuring our vision. Our pilot became disoriented.

The rehearsal was over. Before him was Breezy McLachin's small, pale-green trailer, as the mother had directed him. If the sickly color had not told him, the length of unknotted yellow ribbon hanging limply from the security light would have. He stopped the Jeep and, without hesitation, got out, walked up to the door and knocked. No answer. He knocked once more, louder, and this time a door flung open violently, the one across the way. A well-built woman in her late twenties, in shorts and a red shirt and no shoes, staggered out.

"Don't ever talk to me like that!" came an angry voice from inside, then the man himself, tall, gaunt, red-faced. Riskin watched in stunned surprise as he cocked a fist and slammed it hard against the woman's face. The woman let out an anguished scream. The cry against the still night only opened one other door, to the trailer kitty corner and behind, but it snapped Riskin to. He covered the short distance with the quickness of a fast break up-court, pulled the woman aside and was in her abuser's way before he could take another swing.

"Move aside, boy!" the red-faced man demanded.

"Just who the hell are you?" followed someone else. Riskin shot a glance to his left. It was the couple from the trailer in back.

"I said move aside!" The red-faced man was practically in his face now.

"When you cool down, I'll move," Riskin held his ground.

"Just who the hell appointed you arbitrator?" the guy from the other trailer resumed his line.

"He's probably another one of Breezy's boys," his wife laughed derisively.

"What happened, she throw you out of the Hopper, boy?" the red-faced man taunted, taking another tack.

Riskin cast a look over his shoulder, to the first woman. The whole side of her face was red where the man had hauled off. "Are you all right?" Riskin asked anyway.

UNDER FRIENDLY FIRE

Without a word, she stepped around him, to her husband's side, or whoever the sonofabitch was.

"Go back to the Hopper, boy," the man broke into a toothy grin. "Maybe Breezy's done come around to your number by now."

The man from the other trailer laughed. The woman did not say anything. Neither did Riskin as he turned and left. He could not think of anything appropriate for any of them.

Chapter 3

The Hopper

UNDER FRIENDLY FIRE

THREE

The full name of the place was The Big Hopper. Finding it was not difficult at all. In a town the size of Dexter, you just pointed your pickup truck, or your Jeep, in the direction of most of the lights and all of the noise.

When Riskin arrived, the house band was playing Buddy Holly's *Oh, Boy!* and some girl was taking off her checked shirt and jeans on a table in the middle of the crowded room. From where he stood, far back, her face looked like it belonged on the cover of *Seventeen*. Her body was the most beautiful he had ever seen.

"All of my lovin', all of my kissin', you don't know what you've been a'missin', Oh Boy..."

The girl was down to her bra and panties before Dexter Law stepped up to her table in the six-foot-three, no-neck frame of the shortest crew cut Riskin had ever seen this side of the Persian Gulf. When he helped her down, the women in the place, comparing notes, seemed as disappointed as the men. The men were heartbroken.

Riskin was too numb from the night to be anything. All the same, he leaned forward the two available inches at the bar and asked who the girl on the table was. He got two you-gotta-be-kiddings and one "Who else? Breezy McLachin, the grieving war widow."

The gauntlet just rammed three more feet up his gut. He ordered another beer to calm his abdominal discomfort. Nine out of ten doctors recommended it. The tenth stopped breathing years ago.

"You're not from around here" the guy next to him, around thirty-five, athletic-looking, observed.

Riskin did not feel like talking but he was finding it difficult at such close quarters so he said: "I guess I would've known who she was."

"I guess you would've if you *were* from around here," the man smiled. It was the first genuine smile he had seen since he had arrived in Dexter. "You're a soldier, aren't you?" the man queried out of the blue.

"Was," Riskin replied over the din of voices and clinking glass.

"You were in the Gulf, too, weren't you?"

The guy was being hospitable. Riskin just did not feel like talking about it.

UNDER FRIENDLY FIRE

"No use being humble about it. You fellas did one hell of a job there."

Riskin still did not respond, but the man was not deterred. "And don't even think of paying for another beer. The rest of them are on me," he said.

"Thanks," Riskin finally acknowledged, took a drink of his beer, put the bottle down. "That girl who was up there on the table," he began, craning his neck to see if she were still in place, "wasn't she married to that McLachin who was killed over there?"

"That's right. Did you know him?"

"No, just that--" Riskin had a hard time saying it, "that he got taken out by friendly fire."

"That don't tell you enough about that kid." The man seemed to brace himself on his beer bottle. "McLachin was just about the best damned high school football player in the country."

"The best damned football player," those were the exact words the barber had used to describe McLachin, Riskin recalled through the beer, the smoke. He wondered what this guy could add to that.

"I was his coach at Dexter High," the guy suddenly boasted. What he could add was every conceivable statistic ever recorded on McLachin: career passing yardage, touchdowns thrown, yards rushing, total yardage passing and running for all four years individually. The stats might have bored anyone else, but Riskin still remembered all his own records on the hardcourt. He would never forget them, the same way this guy would always have McLachin's committed to memory. The only problem was bringing him back around to talk about the widow. Riskin did not have to.

"Well, it looks like Breezy's back in uniform again," the man interrupted his own recitation of McLachin's gridiron exploits with a nod beyond Riskin's shoulder.

Turning he saw her at much closer range than before, emerging in her jeans and checked shirt again from the ladies room. The near proximity did nothing to destroy earlier perceptions. Breezy McLachin was stunning. And she was leaving.

As she made her way out, through the mass of nondescript bodies, the band was back on with *Chantilly Lace:* "Hel-looo Ba-by... You know what I like..."

The lead singer's booming impression of the Big Bopper, the amplified guitars and bass made conversation impossible at the bar or anywhere else and Riskin seized the opening. Shaking the coach's hand, he rose from the barstool and took his leave. As he did, the guy said something to him but he could not quite make it out.

Riskin was not certain but it could have been: "Careful."

UNDER FRIENDLY FIRE

Outside the air had chilled considerably when he emerged from The Hopper and it was a whole lot quieter. Too quiet, it abruptly occurred to him as he surveyed the parking lot for sight of her. Then the sound of a door slamming caught his attention. It came from a red pickup in the far corner of the lot. Its dome light was on and he could see two forms inside making out, except one seemed to be carrying the pretense of resistance to new extremes. Riskin broke into a sprint in the direction of the truck. When he reached it, he knew at once his instincts were right. There was no telling how big the punk was who was on top of Breezy McLachin, but it really did not matter. Flinging open the door, he disengaged the guy and lifted him out in one forcible motion. But it was only after the guy was stretched full-length on the pavement from a single roundhouse to his already-fat nose that Riskin was able to calculate his size: Extra Large.

Regaining his own bearings, Riskin turned just in time to almost get run over by the red pickup--with Breezy McLachin behind the wheel.

He tried to call after her but nothing came out.

On the way home she must have stopped off someplace, Riskin figured, because he was waiting for her by her trailer when she got there. As she came up the gravel walk, she carried a six-pack by one empty ring.

"Are you going to let me pass?" she asked simply as he blocked her way.

"Maybe you don't know it, but I did you a favor back there," he unloaded, "and you almost drove your truck right over me."

"Don't take it personal," she shot back.

"Personal?" Riskin was close to being enraged. "What kind of town is this? It's the second time I helped somebody tonight and didn't get diddeley for thanks."

"Sounds like you answered your own question: What kind of town it is." She seemed to look at the other trailers when she said it. "Now are you going to let me pass?"

He let her pass. As she did, she managed to squeeze off one more round: "Seems to me, if you're going to just go around rescuing people, you oughtta get a life of your own, soldier."

Riskin was still standing there a good minute after Breezy McLachin disappeared inside. It was *his* turn to look at the other trailers. They were dark now, and quiet, even the one with the woman who got punched in the face. The red-faced man who did the punching was probably on top of her now, he surmised, and all was right with her world again.

It was not that woman Riskin was thinking of when he walked away, drove down to the ball field he had driven past earlier and, digging out his old Army

UNDER FRIENDLY FIRE

jacket, attempted to get some sleep. As he lay across the first row of the empty grandstand, he tried to dislodge the image of Breezy McLachin from his tired consciousness, not the near-naked one on the tabletop but the dressed and defiant one who had stood a foot away from him in the dark of the trailer park. That was the Breezy McLachin he tried to put out of his mind now.

He did not try too hard.

Chapter 4

Breezy

UNDER FRIENDLY FIRE

FOUR

The soldier-boy was pretty. She could tell he was a soldier by the way he looked, carried himself. Cocky but lost, somehow disoriented. She had noticed him at The Hopper as she left the restroom and was on her way out. She wanted to take a longer look, but she was restless to escape, and *he* was looking at her. Maybe if she had not been thinking about him, it occurred to her, she would have been alert enough to see that big sonofabitch hiding in her truck. It probably saved the bastard's life because she was about to plunge the screwdriver she kept under the seat right between his shoulder blades.

But then the soldier boy might not have come into the picture, might not have been waiting--she stopped. How *did* he know where she was living? Was he a friend of Zed's" From the service maybe, but he was definitely not from around here. She would have seen him before at The Hopper. Sooner or later, they all start hanging out there, usually sooner.

She slipped Zed's old scarlet football jersey over her naked form and wondered why she had driven off, almost running the soldier boy over. If he was not from this neck, she might never have seen him again. Not too smart. But whoever gave Breezy McLachin credit for any smarts except when it came to keeping men's grubby paws off her body, she asked herself. Now *that* took ingenuity, originality.

Zed McLachin's hands had been no different when, as a just-arrived ninth grader at Dexter High, she had won the much vied-for attentions of the school's Mr. Football and Everything Else. Their first clumsy attempts at lovemaking, in the back seat of his father's Buick and the front couch of her absent-as-usual aunt, were best remembered by her for their fervor than for Zed's animal brutality. Sexual abandon was one thing, she thought, but callous self-gratification at the partner's helpless expense smacked of the behavior of serial rapist-murders.

Zed had come a long way from those days, with the help of her intuitive female guidance, a very long way. Their final days together, his last furlough before shipping out to the Gulf, were marked by the most physically fulfilling and yet most tenderly realized lovemaking of their four and a half years together. Never had she wanted a child as much by him as in

UNDER FRIENDLY FIRE

those first painful months he was away, and as much as a manifestation of the new gentler, more caring Zed as for her own maternal longings.

It was not to be.

Breezy McLachin propped up the two pillows, reached for a beer can on the nightstand, tilted her head back. For some reason, it seemed, the light overhead shone dimmer. But lights do not dim before they burn out. They die all of a sudden. Like her parents in the station wagon and like Zed in the War.

Random thoughts checked off. Her father used to drink beer in bed. After the accident, she herself became afraid of the dark. The first six times she and Zed made love it was in the daylight. He reintroduced her to the darkness. In their marriage, especially that final leave, it became their own special place of hiding, refuge, that only the two of them knew about and shared.

"They can't get us now," Zed would whisper as they lay together. "They can't get us because they don't know where we are."

She never understood who *they* were. *Then* she could not understand. Now, in the months following the telegram, she thought she was beginning to know.

For most of his twenty-two years, people had made demands of Zed McLachin's time, his privacy, his life. Being the star football player in a fishbowl the size of Dexter was at once the best and the worst thing *that* ever happened to him. She had always felt it was the real reason he never really considered the offers from Tennessee and Alabama, that he joined the Marines, rather than be subjected to more of the same kind of public scrutiny but worse because it would be on a national scale.

The escape worked. It worked until he would return to Dexter, then the scrutiny, the smothering would start all over again, in spades. From friends, from people who wanted desperately to be, from the faithful followers of Dexter football who would never forget or let *him* forget, from everybody in this tiny, stifling, one-horse town, but most especially Luke McLachin.

If Luke McLachin could have stayed in the Marines the rest of his natural life, he would have been the happiest, most miserable man on earth. If he had not been told in the bluntest of terms to get the hell out, Zed McLachin may well have coped with his local celebrity and even gone on to star for the Volunteers or Crimson Tide. Running Prospect Trailer Park was part-time work for military retirees. Being Zed's father and chief trophy polisher was not.

Now, after Zed's death, the attention had shifted. Not the pressure because that had always been there, the worse from Luke McLachin and his rubber-stamp wife Lenora, but now even that "civic responsibility" had become more intense, more focused. Before, she

UNDER FRIENDLY FIRE

had been the wife of a High School All-American and Dexter's most colorful, seemingly freest spirit. Now she was the widow of a legend.

Death does that, she said to herself sardonically as she finished her beer, replaced the can on the night table. The light above her *was* getting dimmer. Either that or she was finally getting too tired to stay awake, to keep remembering, and wishing the light was not on at all and he was with her where *they* could not get them because they did not have a clue where to look.

The light was still on in the morning. The sun shining through the trailer's small bedroom window only made it look like it was out. The pillows, her head were still propped up as she glanced at the clock. It read six-thirty exactly. What an amazing gift, she smiled sleepily. To wake at precisely the same time everyday without the aid of an alarm. She wondered if such a talent might land her a guest spot on Letterman.

But the other was an even greater gift. To party, to have as many beers as she had had the night before, and the night before that, and not feel a thing, not even the most minuscule of headaches. She marveled at the restorative powers of sleep, three and a half hours of it.

In fifteen minutes she was showered and dressed, in another ten behind the counter of Ted's Dexter

MICHAEL CORNELL

Diner. Since 1968, before that the Dexter Diner since, as the joke went, 1492.

"I heard two things," Ted Bolan was saying through the kitchen's meal-waiting window.
"Tell me one," Breezy McLachin peered through the opening.
"That you were dancing buck-naked on a table at The Hopper last night."
"Just a good story. Next."
"The barber was just in here for his usual late supper and says a GI who knew Zed was looking for you."
"Yeah, and a fat slob was waiting for me last night in my truck."
"Trouble?"
"I didn't rape him if that's what you mean."
"Customer," Bolan abruptly announced.
"Ted, I swear you're the only person I know whose hearing gets better with age," Breezy kidded and turned from the serving window.
At the far end of the counter was Soldier Boy.

Chapter 5

Interim

UNDER FRIENDLY FIRE

FIVE

A whirring noise stirred Jimmy Riskin from his fitful sleep on the hard grandstand. Looking up, he saw an orange pickup with some sort of buffer attachment smoothing out the all-dirt infield of the baseball diamond.

"Sorry to wake you, buddy," the guy in the truck called out above the drone, "but the dust is going to get you if you don't move. There's an early game today-- before it gets too hot."

Riskin rubbed his eyes, sat upright, then rose and made his way groggily to the public restrooms to relieve himself and wash up. When he returned to his Jeep, he changed shirts and asked the guy the best place to have breakfast.

"Don't have a lotta choice here, but I'd say the Dexter Diner on Main." Then he added as an afterthought: "That is, if you don't mind eating your heart out."

Riskin did not pursue that, just thanked the man and headed off on foot, leaving the Jeep parked in foul territory well beyond third base.

Five minutes later, when he saw Breezy McLachin behind the counter, he understood what the guy in the pickup meant. Even on an empty stomach, it was tough thinking about food. And, as she approached, the faint rustling of her legs against the thin material of her short uniform told him it was not going to get any easier.

"Coffee?"

"Coffee?" Riskin tried to stay calm. "Don't you remember me--from last night?"

"That was last night. Life goes on."

"For you, life almost didn't."

"For me, maybe it stopped some time ago. Now may I take your order?"

"I've got to talk to you," It sounded more desperate than he wanted.

"Zed's dead," she said suddenly. "Now pick a number."

"Pick a number?"

"From 1 to 5," she pointed to the menu board.

"One," he spit out.

She was headed back toward the kitchen. And people were starting to come in. He would never be able to talk to her now.

UNDER FRIENDLY FIRE

Zed's dead. I know that you stuckup bitch, I was the one who blew him away. Dexter, The Friendliest City in the U.S.A. What a joke. He would eat his breakfast, Riskin decided, and get the hell out of the Friendliest City in the U.S.A.

She returned with his order, put the check down.

"I get off at three-thirty," Breezy McLachin said quietly, then turned to go take another order.

Riskin could not down the meal fast enough. He wanted to be out of there. Most of all, he did not want to look at her while he ate; his heart would beat that much faster, harder if he did. His thoughts--if something as confused, as incoherent could be called thinking--made him angry, not at her anymore, but himself. He had to talk to her. She had finally agreed. He had not asked her out for a drink, for dinner. What he had to discuss was not the stuff of candlelight dinners. So why did his chest feel like it was going to explode, his throat feel as dry as it did even with steaming coffee pouring down it, and his empty stomach seem to be rejecting anything he stuck in it? If he knew those answers, he said, he would also know why his head felt even more light-headed than the beers had made it feel last night. And he would know why he felt like bursting out laughing and falling on his face on somebody's new-mowed lawn, like the old song went.

MICHAEL CORNELL

    He finished, paid his bill without looking at her and twice replaced older bills with newer ones when he left her tip.
    At the ball field, a Little League game was in the third inning. He arrived just in time to see a chunky red-haired kid put a long foul ball off the hood of his Jeep.
    "You gotta park it farther away than that, soldier," called out the coach of the green team. Riskin recognized him at once as the friendly guy at The Hopper from the night before, the only one. "We got some kids who can really jerk 'em here."
    "What's another dent," Riskin shrugged. "I quit counting a long time ago."
    "Good," the man smiled, then seemed to stare at him for a stretch as he approached the bench on the way out to left field and his Jeep. "The name's Tim Holt, same as that old cowboy star," the man extended a hand, "and I know a fella who's played some ball."
    "A little."
    "Uh-uh. More than a little," the guy said knowingly, then turned to his team of green uniforms riding the bench. "All right, listen up: I gotta take care of some business. I'll try to be back, but while I'm gone, this is your interim manager."
    Riskin was floored on his feet. He did not know what to say.

UNDER FRIENDLY FIRE

"What's interim?" one of the kids chirped up in a squeaky tone.

"Does he got a name?" another asked.

"Jimmy Riskin," he answered, then wondered why *that* was the first thing he said instead of why me.

"Does this game got a score?"

"Five to nothing," the squeaky one replied. "Them."

Holt put a friendly hand on his shoulder. "I'm a sore loser, see, but maybe you can do better. I've skippered these runts too long; they don't listen to me anymore. But wait 'til I get 'em in high school."

Riskin watched him saunter away, still too tongue-tied to say more than he already had. A solid crack of the bat roused him out of it. Turning, he saw another fly arch toward left, hook foul and strike his Jeep on the hood, just below the windshield.

"Told you these runts can jack 'em," Holt called back from the low exit gate and laughed. "War is hell, ain't it?"

Riskin laughed back, turned his attention to the game. The kid who jacked the long foul struck out swinging on the next pitch. A nice off-speed pitch. Or a slow fastball. He could not tell which. He just congratulated the skinny kid in the green uniform who threw it when the side was out.

"I'm Jimmy Riskin," he reintroduced himself to the ones who had been playing the field and were now coming up to bat. "I've known Mr. Holt a *long* time," he lied, "and when he comes back, I want us to be out in front in this game, do you hear?"

"Did you see *their* pitcher?" the catcher slumped down.

"Their pitcher throws thirty-five in a forty zone," Riskin returned without even looking out at the opposing hurler's warm-up tosses.

"Fastest thirty-five I ever faced," an over-sized kid with glasses smirked.

"The faster it goes, the sweeter it feels when you kiss it," Riskin followed up and wondered where the words came from. Tim Holt maybe, he smiled to himself, the cowboy.

"Let's nuke 'em, Dexter!" somebody bellowed from behind. Turning, Riskin was surprised to see the green-capped grandmotherly-type who had yelled out, and thirty-five, forty other adults, mostly family, sitting and watching. He had not noticed them at all when he entered the park. He resolved not to notice them again. It was the most beautiful day since his discharge, the sky was a Crayola baby-blue, and he was determined to win one for Tim Holt, wherever he was saddled up.

Four innings later, Riskin was still staring at a deficit, but one run instead of five. He was also confronted with the kind of rookie manager's nightmare of a decision that made him wish Holt had

UNDER FRIENDLY FIRE

returned to take him off the hook. A bad-hop grounder had loaded the bases and put the potential tying and winning runs at second and third. The situation would have been golden had it not been for the kid Riskin had coming up. The boy had the pale, delicate handsomeness of a child-prodigy pianist, not the reckless, let-me-end-this-thing look or demeanor of a kid who just might make good on such juvenile bravado and smack one fair, past his Jeep and everything else.

To make things worse, the Dexter faithful in the grandstand behind him was letting him know they did not want little Van Cliburn to bat, but a pinch hitter instead. Naturally, they all seemed to be yelling for a different kid to perform the honors, but looking down the bench, even Riskin had to admit that the relaxed abandon he was looking for was more evident in the scrubs riding pine, than in the child-prodigy with the bat in his hands. What's more, the thin-limbed boy had whiffed the last time up on three pitches.

Riskin called a time-out, signaled his little batter back to the on-deck circle. Close-up, his sensitive eyes seemed to heap even more insecurity upon the impending circumstances.

"Take 'im out," yelled some callous loud-mouth from the stands. Others took up the chant, nominating their own choices for potential glory.

MICHAEL CORNELL

Riskin tried to block the voices out of his head, but he saw the futile impossibility of the boy doing the same.

"How do you feel?" Riskin asked him.

"Scared," the boy said honestly, his voice breaking.

Riskin threw a reluctant glance back at the grandstand, catching the impassioned faces at a Little League baseball game so far from Yankee Stadium or the MetroDome, that he could vomit.

"Nothing to be scared about," he told the boy. "Watch the ball. Their pitcher's lost some smoke. He's tired. Watch the ball and just meet it."

"I'll try."

"That's all you can do," Riskin said, then added: "And don't pay any attention to the people in the stands. Remember, you got someone out there who thinks you can do it."

"My Mom's sitting in the first row, but I guess she's not too loud," the boy looked past him with his sad, frightened eyes.

"I'm not talking about your Mom," Riskin smiled. "I'm talking about me."

The boy's pale face seemed to color, lighten up. He headed for home plate.

Riskin could not recall a sweeter sound than the sound that thirty-one ounce bat made. It was better than stereo. Better than Dolby. But as sweet as it was, it only tied the sight of the ball falling fair down the

UNDER FRIENDLY FIRE

right field line. A flare for anybody else. A screaming rope for little Van Cliburn.

"I want to thank you," came the quiet, refined voice behind the quiet, sensitive eyes, eyes he had seen only moments before. Someone else's eyes. "I'm Brandon's mother."

"Your son gets the credit," Riskin replied, then reproached himself for the trite-sounding remark.

"My son shouldn't have batted," the woman said and, for the first time, he saw how beautiful she was. Not like Breezy was beautiful, but different, with every strand of auburn hair in place and makeup so subtly applied it did not seem to be there at all. "There were thirty-some screaming idiots up there telling you Brandon shouldn't be batting."

"Well then, aren't you glad the interim coach was too much of an idiot to know that?" The response was something that just occurred to him, but *this* time he liked the sound of it.

"I hope you'll be staying in Dexter awhile," she smiled, then turned to locate her son in the boisterous mob that had swallowed him up. Riskin stared after her. Even her curves were quiet, refined, like a porcelain figure that would break if you touched it.

Looking at her, he suddenly felt dirty. He had the compulsion to shower and shave, plant himself in some Motel 6 room that had a bed with blankets, clean sheets, and a mattress softer than the weathered seats of his dented-up Jeep.

He had an even stronger compulsion for it to be three-thirty. It was ten after ten. Three-thirty seemed years away. A year anyway. Tim Holt was riding the range again, oblivious of the stirring Little League victory, Breezy McLachin was probably serving eggs sunny-side-up-gone-bad to some hairy truck driver with no sleeves, and Jimmy Riskin was stuck in some damned time warp with a military-issue wrist watch that kept reading ten after ten.

It was good to be back in the world again, he thought.

Chapter 6

Crazy

◻

UNDER FRIENDLY FIRE

SIX

It was not a Motel 6. It was the Rustic Motor Inn. The room was no more than the place's name, decorated in Early-'60's American Motel with real paintings, probably purchased at a "Starving Artists" sale, guaranteed to keep them starving for years to come. Still, the bedspreads were clean and the linen new. The television was an old black-and-white Philco, but the shower faucet advertised Hot and Cold and made good on the claim. The one major deterrent was the distance Riskin had to travel from Dexter to get there: a good six miles, nearly to the interstate. It was one way to discourage visitors to your town, he thought. No, McDonalds was the other. People who stopped at the Rustic could avail themselves of the motel's own bar and grill, a quirky log relic straight out of Edward Hopper, that looked less inviting than the description would promise.

MICHAEL CORNELL

Riskin lay on the bed in his underwear, feeling clean and whole once more, and determined not to look at his watch again on the night table, until the hour hand started budging with noticeable change. He closed his eyes and began reviewing a would-be dialogue for informing Breezy of the unfortunate events of a few months before. At some point, his eyelids became heavier and the surroundings ceased to exist. In their place was a blinding blizzard of finely granulated sand. Every so often a crevice would crack in the driving sand wall, and he could spy light, not electric, but more the illumination of fireworks, brightly colored and loud in its combustion. There were voices as well, shouting of some sort, but their source was multi-directional with no way of tracking their actual origins. The entire effect was one of confusion, chaos on a big-screen scale. Suddenly, there was one deafening explosion and the sand wall was obliterated into white-yellow nothingness.

His eyes were open again, his body poised as he now sat up. He raised his hand to his forehead and it was still dry. Even that seemed understandable because, through it all, he had never really been scared. The experience was reminiscent of going through a funhouse at a carnival. You were startled momentarily at every unexpected turn, but you knew sooner or later you were coming out into the daylight again so you

UNDER FRIENDLY FIRE

really could not have been that scared at all. Only enough to get your money's worth.

Riskin reached over to the night table. The small hand on his wristwatch had moved appreciably. The time read 2:48. He swung his feet to the floor, dressed, rechecked the watch. It read 2:53. Five minutes, most of which he had spent looking through his duffel bag for the least-wrinkled shirt. He sat on the edge of the bed and tried to remember the last time he got this psyched up to see a woman. He could not. There would not have been a comparison anyway, he derided himself for trying. The last time he was not getting ready to tell the woman he had killed her husband.

The last time the woman did not look like Breezy McLachin.

When he got to the diner and peered inside from his Jeep at 3:26, Riskin felt like a fool. There were two other ones joking and shooting the breeze--appropriately enough--with her from across the counter. She had that kind of way with men, reducing all of them to slobbering idiots. All but Jimmy Riskin, he gritted his teeth.

No. Jimmy Riskin included. He hopped out of the Jeep, went inside.

"I heard that one before, boys," she was saying to her two ogling admirers, both obvious locals, "but better. I tell it better."

MICHAEL CORNELL

Riskin took a seat in a booth close to the front door.

"Got company, fellas," Breezy told the two. They looked over with something more than passing interest as she came from around the counter.

"Don't take any candy from strangers," Breezy, one of them said.

"It's not what you think, boys," she shook her head on the way over, "he was a friend of my husband."

"Them are the worst kind," the other opined.

"Don't mind them," Breezy was standing over him now.

"Mind who?" Riskin smiled.

"What was that you said?" the first guy at the counter called over.

"Town's got keen hearing," Riskin observed wryly.

"From miles away," she rolled her eyes almost imperceptibly. "You still think this is a good idea?"

"Unless you got a better one."

"How 'bout not at all?"

"That's not a better one," came his return. It did not seem to do anything for her--or her two pals who had joined them. The pair just stood there looking, chewing on toothpicks, different ones, but it might as well have been the same one, the way they were butted up against each other in their matching, faded denims.

UNDER FRIENDLY FIRE

"Fellas, this is--"

"Jim Riskin," he filled in the blank.

"Nice to meet you," one or both of them nodded; he could not tell. In either case, the tone was not the cordial Chamber of Commerce opener.

"Gonna be here long" the first one asked.

"Not if the hospitality doesn't improve," Riskin replied matter-of-factly.

"Good," the second one said.

"Hospitality is something you earn around here," the first one grinned, baring broken teeth. He either had a bad dentist or was a born hockey player. "Remember what I said about taking candy from strangers, Breezy. Don't think Zed would approve. Seeya."

The pair left as one.

"Where Zed is, he ain't approvin' or disapprovin' anything," she said after the door closed. "I'll get my things and meet you in back."

"We can take mine," he offered.

"Leave it where it is. I like to know where I'm going," she shot back over her shoulder.

In five minutes, they were on the two-laner to the Interstate, but faster. The only time she let up on the pickup truck's accelerator, on a straight-away, was to pull her waitress uniform over her head and off. Riskin looked away on reflex.

MICHAEL CORNELL

"Do I bother you?" she raised her voice over the engine. "Is that why you look away?"

"I looked away because you don't bother me at all." Riskin glared across at her in her skimpy silk slip.

"Good. Then you can reach under the seat and give me that plastic bag," she called back.

He did and she removed a little apricot-colored mini from it, slipped it on without removing the one hand from the wheel or slowing under forty-five.

"I'm impressed," Riskin let her know.

"With my driving?"

"That too."

The speedometer was back up to sixty-five, seventy. She did not reduce it until she took the turn into the Rustic Motor Inn's gravel parking lot.

"I'm staying here," Riskin said with frank surprise.

"Well, don't get any ideas," Breezy curled her lip, turned off the engine. "You let me get the ideas, okay?"

All he could say was: "Okay."

They headed for the bar and grill. He was not leading the way. He was too confused, too disarmed to be leading anyone. Or too disarmed to be more than confused. Riskin could buy either, but he brought her a beer instead. He half-expected her to drink from the bottle.

56

UNDER FRIENDLY FIRE

"Thanks," she said, pouring it into a glass, and suddenly she was a sixteen-year-old taking her first taste of beer. Riskin felt lucky being the first one to corrupt her, he laughed to himself.

"You're very pretty," he heard himself say for the very first time in his life, then questioned who the *real* sixteen-year-old was at their table.

"Thank you," she acknowledged the compliment as though it were the very first time *she* had heard it. "I'm glad you brought me here to tell me."

The tone was the same, but the drift was there, he was certain of it.

"I'm sorry," he started over, "I wanted to talk to you about your husband."

"I'm sorry too," she grimaced. "Let's get some music in here."

She left the booth, went over to the old stained-glass jukebox and inserted all her change. Riskin could not see her selections, but, from where he sat, he was more than encouraged. Watching her in front of the colored light made him think of *Shake, Rattle and Roll*. "You wear those dresses and the sun'll come shinin' through..." He lowered his head, chuckled in his beer. When was he ever going to get those rock 'n' roll lyrics out of his old crash helmet, he wondered. When he started reading Heinlein, he answered himself.

MICHAEL CORNELL

Patsy Cline had a better idea. *Crazy* was playing when Breezy returned to the table. It made as much sense as anything else. She was now seated on *his* side of the booth.

"You're very pretty." she half-whispered. Riskin could not tell if she were mimicking him or what. It must have shown in his face, because she proceeded on: "You are, you know. But you know that already, don't you, soldier boy?"

If she had got up on the tabletop at that very moment, as she had the night before, at The Hopper, it would have not surprised him. He would not have stopped her either, so he did the first logical thing he could think of: He took a drink of his beer. It was his first. The second followed at once.

"You must think I'm evil," Breezy smiled evilly.

"Something like that," he managed, "but don't stop."

The next thing she did was even crazier: She got up from the table.

"You didn't know Zed at all, you lyin' sonofabitch!" she spat out after the door slammed.

By the time he reached the parking lot, her pickup truck was a memory. Twice in two nights. It was a pretty good average.

Chapter 7

Ginny

UNDER FRIENDLY FIRE

SEVEN

Bastard.

Jim Riskin no more knew her husband than she played bridge with Elizabeth Taylor every Thursday or any other day. Breezy pressed the pedal all the way to the floor. The needle mounted swiftly, then just as abruptly, began its descent. The lights of the trailer park were now in view. In a matter of seconds, she was negotiating the turn into it, driving up to Luke and Lenora's.

The woman must have heard the truck. She was at the door before Breezy could mount the two small metal steps.

"Lenora, did you tell some pretty-boy soldier where the hell he could find me?" Breezy demanded to know.

"But, dear, he already knew if he came this far," Mrs. McLachin answered diffidently.

"Then he *did* stop by to see you?" Breezy continued in her rancor.

"Yes, but he said he knew Zachary."

"Like hell he did!"

"Then how did he get *your* name?" the woman inquired with no additional courage.

"How should I know. Maybe Zed was flashing my damn picture around over there, showing me off."

"That's because he was proud of you," Mrs. McLachin smiled feebly.

Breezy had not heard what she said. Another voice, coming from beyond the door, caught her by surprise, stopped her dead.

Zed's.

She pushed past the woman, into the living room. He was there. Luke McLachin was watching him on the television screen.

"Remember this interview of Zed after he threw the three touchdown passes in the state high school football tournament?" the man glanced at her over his huge shoulder. "Coach Holt got a copy of it for me."

"But why are you watching it now?" Breezy asked.

"Why am I watching it?" McLachin struck a puzzled look at his wife.

"Yes, why are you watching it *now?*" Breezy ignored their unspoken accord in the matter.

UNDER FRIENDLY FIRE

"I'm watching it because Zed is my damn flesh and blood, that's why!" the man raised his voice above the television.

Lenora McLachin attempted to smooth things out in her usual ineffectual tone: "Luke dear, Breezy is our guest, you know."

"Guest?" her husband dismissed her weak attempt. "She lives in the same damn trailer park we do."

"Well... maybe she would like to watch Zachary's and her wedding instead," the woman stumbled on. "We got that on tape, too."

Breezy looked at her, at him, back at her without saying a word.

"Is there something wrong?" Mrs. McLachin queried with honest concern.

Breezy's response had the same honesty. She left, closing the door quietly behind her.

At the door of her own trailer, she found she could not step inside, could not even touch the door handle. Instead, she walked around to the back and looked across the field of tall grass that extended to the distant, sloping hills to Ginny Walker's.

Thank God Ginny was there. But Ginny was always there.

"You come a long way, Breezy, on a day like this," the elderly black woman greeted her, "so you musta had a good reason."

MICHAEL CORNELL

Breezy stepped inside, felt the shack's warmth at once. Everything was the same as it had always been, the colorful African tapestries on the bare-board walls, the old green Coke bottles hanging over the small paneless windows, the card table with one lame leg.

"Sit," the old woman motioned toward the card table. The two of them took their places in rickety chairs at right angles from each other. "Tell Ginny your good reason for bein' here."

"I'm confused," Breezy said candidly. "While Zed was alive, I felt all kinds of forces, pressures on me. Now that he's gone, I still feel as though I'm being bombarded with other kinds of forces, demands on me. Sometimes I want to break wide open, tell everybody to just go to hell."

"And do you seriously think anybody would listen to you if you did?" Ginny smiled her beautiful toothless grin.

"Maybe they wouldn't," Breezy answered, leaning back in the chair and hearing it creak, "but it sure would release whatever it is that's pent up inside me."

"We all got things welled up in us," Ginny shook her white-haired head, "the trouble is, in a town the size of Dexter, there ain't no place you can go up on a hill and shout the devil out of you except maybe The Point--and *that's* somebody's private property."

"Then maybe, Ginny, I don't belong in Dexter no more, now that Zed's on the *other* hill."

UNDER FRIENDLY FIRE

"Maybe you don't."

Breezy watched her weary form get up from the table, go to the battered steel cupboard, take out a gallon milk-bottle filled with what looked like papaya juice. She brought it back to the table with two immaculately clean glasses and poured juice in each of them. Breezy tasted hers. It was a cross between papaya and pineapple and tasted delicious.

"Maybe you don't," Ginny repeated herself, "but there's somethin' more that's eatin' at you or you wouldn't be here talkin' to me about it."

Breezy smiled. "Do you know me or what?" she laughed quietly.

"And if my instincts serve me at all," the old woman resumed, "this quand'ry you're wrastlin' with has somethin' to do with a man. Well, I ain't even gonna bother to ask you his name or who he is or nothin'; I'm just gonna ask you how long you been thinkin' about him."

"I just met him yesterday," Breezy was reluctant to admit.

"That don't matter none," Ginny emitted a wheezy chuckle, "sometimes that's more 'n enough. It just seems to you he's been stuck inside your head for a lot longer than that, huh?"

Breezy nodded.

"Keep him inside there," Ginny advised in her grandmotherly way. "Don't lock him out. If he's worth anything worth anything, he'll stay put in there and you'll know what to do."

Breezy took another drink of juice, leaned back again. It was more than delicious.

"Now what say you get out of them things you're wearing and lay on the bed," the old woman suggested. "A good rub-dub will loosen up some of those forces you been feelin'."

Breezy started removing her clothes as the old woman returned to the metal cupboard and removed a thick brown salad bowl. She began mixing mineral oil and milk in it. As she did, a gentle breeze tinkled the empty Coke bottles like chimes.

In minutes, Breezy felt hands kneading her skin with a soothing pressure that belied their boniness. It seemed as though she could count every individual finger, each smoothing out, assuaging the very fiber of her being. The events of the late afternoon quickly became somebody else's unpleasant experiences, not hers. Luke and Lenora McLachin, even Riskin for now, were somebody else's nemeses, not the problems of a deity such as herself who had her own court counsel, her very own masseuse.

"Your trouble's just gonna float away," a voice called out at a great distance. As she listened for it again, she now felt what seemed like twice, three times as many milky, probing fingers roaming over her weightless, floating body.

UNDER FRIENDLY FIRE

"Your trouble's just gonna fly away."

Hands now turned her over on her stomach. Gentle, caring hands with busy, caressing fingers. Gentler than Zed's had ever been. Far off, she now heard the funny sound of a baby's bottom being spanked, not with mean-spirited brusqueness but with good-natured affection. There were more spanks to either side, the deep silence, tranquility.

At some point, Breezy felt herself being lifted from her cushioned cloud, placed in a shallow pool of warm, friendly water. Once more, hands resumed their happy work, squeezing, lathering.

When she opened her eyes, she was still nude, except now she was seated at the crooked card table with Ginny Walker. Instinctively, Breezy lifted her arms to cover her breasts. The old woman just shook her head with peaceful calm. She lowered her arms.

Ginny reached into a small, weathered burlap pouch, withdrew three wooden Scrabble tiles, one by one. Breezy watched her emancipated fingers place them down atop the card table. They read I-M-J.

Breezy extended her smooth bare arm, rearranged them.

What they spelled made her shiver.

Chapter 8

Whitney

UNDER FRIENDLY FIRE

EIGHT

The gash was a good four inches long, just above the wheel rim. Dents on the hood from long foul balls were one thing, Jimmy Riskin shook his head angrily, slashed tires were another. He glared inside the diner. Breezy McLachin was not working this morning. He would change the tire, have it replaced, then go see her one last time, dammit, and get the hell out of Dexter forever. Again.

"Trouble, son?" He looked up to see the oversized, uniformed skinhead who had preempted the exciting conclusion to Breezy's table-top striptease two nights before. His large, wind-burned elbow stuck out of Dexter's police car, its only one, Riskin was sure. "Shouldn't park it there overnight. Where was you stayin', anyway?"

"The Rustic," he answered civilly.

"Last time I was there, they had themselves a parking lot," the lawman cracked. "How'd you get back to town?"

"A salesman from Kansas City gave me a lift."

"Nice town Kansas City. Real friendly. Kansas or Missouri?"

"I forgot to ask him," Riskin said, yanking the hubcap off with the Jeep's tire-iron.

"Well, I hope you didn't forget to thank him," crewcut laughed, drove off. Riskin watched the car turn the corner for no good reason, then finished changing the tire.

The old-time filling station, like the Rustic's bar and grill, was also out of Edward Hopper. White wood siding, red-shingled roof, with the last old-style round pumps in America. There the manager, an affable guy with one whole side of his face burned red, sold him a used spare. As he mounted it on the Jeep's tailgate the fellow kept his Atlanta Brave-capped head buried behind the forward-opening red hood of a vintage Jaguar XKE convertible. Nice machine, he thought, wonder who owns it. He finished mounting the tire, wandered over.

"Start it up," the guy in the baseball cap said. Riskin slid behind the wheel, turned the key. "Now run the engine...more," the man directed. Riskin gunned it some, listened, switched off the motor.

UNDER FRIENDLY FIRE

"It's an easy one," he called out over the raised hood. "The distributor. I'd look at the induction coil, too. If it's the original, it probably should be replaced."

"Where'd you learn so much about Jaguars, kid?" The man came around to the driver's side, wiping his hands on his coveralls.

"My dad brought back one from England when he was stationed there for six months," Riskin replied. "It wasn't an XKE, just an old closed coupe, but all their electrical was screwed up. Most English cars were."

"Your dad was in the Army?" the guy inquired. When Riskin nodded, he seemed to think it over a spell, then said: "Take a look at this one over here."

Riskin got out of the Jaguar, followed the man over to a pale-yellow Plymouth Reliant.

"Start it up." He opened the door for Riskin who got in, fired the car up. It was racing terribly.

"What year is this?" Riskin wanted to know.

"'Eighty-five."

"Another easy one," Riskin smiled. "It was the last year of the normally aspirated carburetor, before they switched completely over to fuel injection on all the models."

"Prescription?"

"Adjust the idle and pray a lot," Riskin smirked.

"Eight bucks," the guy asserted.

"Eight bucks?"

"An hour."

Riskin laughed. Out of the blue, the offer struck him funny. He said: "Sorry."

"Ten then," the station manager countered. "Thirty hours a week to start."

Riskin was still smirking. The notion of staying on in Dexter, the Friendliest City in the U.S.A., was a cruel joke. "Sorry," he reiterated.

"Good morning." A third voice had joined them. A low, smooth cultured one he had heard before. Riskin turned to see the pretty woman from the Little League game.

"Good morning," he returned her friendliness.

"You two know each other?" The guy in the baseball cap was genuinely surprised.

"All he did was make a big hero out of my little Brandon," she declared.

"Your son was holding the bat," Riskin took a dumb stab at humility.

"And who was to blame for that?"

"I give," he smiled.

"So you've decided to give our little town a chance?" she asked.

"I tried to offer him--" the man attempted to interject before Riskin cut him off.

UNDER FRIENDLY FIRE

"Well, as a matter of fact, I just agreed to stay on to help out at the station here," Riskin surprised them all, including himself.

"I'm delighted to hear that," the woman said, looking at him with the kind of feminine warmth he had not seen since before the Gulf.

"He's even diagnosed your Jag's problem," his new boss boasted. "We'll have to order the parts, but in the meantime you can drive it."

"Well not today I can't," she informed them, indicating the minivan idling nearby. "Like all the other mothers in Dexter, I drive one of *those* to school and Little League. But when I want to feel free and crazy again, I drive the red Jaguar."

"I'll have my *new* mechanic deliver it to the house this morning," the fellow in the baseball cap announced, patting Riskin on the arm.

"Oh, not this morning, one o'clock this afternoon," the woman said as she headed back to her minivan. "I'll be home then."

Riskin liked the way she smiled at him. It would keep until one o'clock easy.

"You're something, kid," the man removed his baseball cap, wiped his bald head as the minivan drove off. "You just arrive in Dexter a day, whatever, and you're friendly with the Mayor's wife right from the get-go."

The Mayor's wife. The words jumped out at him. Someone had already mentioned her to him--it was the barber, he now recalled--and said she was a former beauty queen or something once. *That* made sense, he thought; on the other hand, staying on might not have been such a good idea after all.

"Well, how about it," the guy broke his train, "you wantta start this morning?"

"Why not," he shrugged his shoulders.

"Good," the man nodded, putting his cap back on. "Nice to have a smart mechanic around here again, helps business. Had one once, a real whiz, big strapping kid who'd spend a lotta time around military motor pools. Was a helluva football player, too. Poor kid died in the Gulf War. Boy named McLachin, Zed McLachin."

That's just it, Riskin said to himself, Zed *wasn't* dead. He would never die.

The irony lingered for the next few hours. Now he was even working in the same place as Zed McLachin had worked, probably using the same damned socket wrenches Zed had used. He was relieved to be asking Flaherty, his boss, for directions to the Mayor's house to deliver the Jaguar. It did not matter that he did not know the Mayor's name, or his wife's, only their son Brandon's. He had had his fill of the name Zed McLachin for the day.

UNDER FRIENDLY FIRE

To call the Mayor's house a house was tantamount to saying Nolan Ryan's fastball was pretty fast. The estate, complete with wrought-iron gate and winding drive, looked like Tara, The Economy Model but impressive the same. Riskin parked the Jaguar and was greeted by an old-time black maid who had him wait in the seemingly cavernous foyer. On the walls hung real paintings, something Riskin knew little about except for some Edward Hopper and some Remington Western art an Army roommate from the East had introduced him to. Coming from somewhere he could not detect, quiet classical piano was being piped in. *That* was something he knew even less about, except for some Van Cliburn Tchaikovsky the same roomie would play when he got drunk.

The maid returned to inform him that Mrs. Fallon--so that was her name--would see him in the Georgia room. He wondered if that were just outside the Florida room city limits.

"Thank you for bringing the car," Mrs. Fallon extended a long alabaster hand. In it was a mauve-colored envelope. "Here's a little something for your kindness."

He raised his hand at the wrist, said: "Mr. Flaherty says you can pay when the parts come in and we install them."

"Then *you* take it," she insisted, "for what you did for Brandon yesterday."

75

"Look," he shook his head, "he could've struck out. As it was, he got a hit. I was as happy as you were. It won us the game."

"All right," she withdrew the envelope, "but you can't refuse the iced tea Ethel already fixed for you." She indicated the tall glass on an Oriental tray on the antique side-table nearby. Riskin took it with a grateful nod, looked around the room for some sign of Georgia. The closest he came was the expensive-looking pastel peach wallpaper. The rest was porcelain ballerinas and glass music boxes.

"What brings you to Dexter?" Mrs. Fallon now had her own tall glass, still full.

"I came to see someone," he answered.

"And whom might that be?"

"Well, I still haven't seen them yet," he said in something short of a lie.

"All right," Mrs. Fallon changed her tack, "then where have you come from?"

"From the War in the Gulf."

"It was a remarkable show," she beamed with good intention, but he could not help himself: "We had other terms for it, equally descriptive." He took a long drink of his iced tea, all he wanted.

"I didn't mean to pass it off so lightly," she apologized with real sincerity. "I know it must have been very frightening."

UNDER FRIENDLY FIRE

What was it about rooms and houses like this that intimidated him so easily, so effectively, he asked himself, but said: "I've really got to get back, Mrs. Fallon. I think Mr. Flaherty has already put the notice out because, as I left, cars making funny noises and one pickup not making any noise at all pulled up to the service bay."

"Well, then can I at least drive you back to town?"

"Mr. Flaherty should be waiting by the front gate by now in his tow truck. Thanks anyway."

She was genuinely disappointed. He could tell.

"Listen," Mrs. Fallon made one last try, "my husband will be out of town next week at a convention of small-town mayors, an exercise in male bonding. If you'd like, I'd love to show you around the area. There's more to it than meets the eye."

"That would be nice," he accepted more readily than he had any sense to.

Flaherty was waiting by the front gate. Riskin was glad to be getting out of there, but sorry to be leaving.

Chapter 9

Confession

UNDER FRIENDLY FIRE

NINE

Jimmy Riskin felt like one of them. He had accepted the job offer at the filling station and now, his first night off, he was at The Hopper looking for somebody to have a beer with. That somebody was not Breezy McLachin, a dead end, *or* Mrs. Fallon, a no-win, his second thoughts told him, someone else's wife. She would never go there anyway. Riskin was looking for Tim Holt, the coach not the cowboy, and he was there at the bar where he had been the other night.

"Sure, upstage me and win the damn ball game," Holt opened up at once when he saw him coming over. "Can't leave you with a five-run spot without you bringing 'em back!"

"Hey, next time leave me even, okay?" Riskin volleyed, "but *this* time buy me a beer."

"You pull that comeback stunt again, pal, and I'll buy you a beer truck," Holt laughed as he signalled for two from the bartender. The house band was on their break and it felt good to be able to hear what was being said, to carry on a conversation, and Holt was carrying on the conversation: "Next week: summer football workouts. I need a halfback coach."

"You need a halfback coach who'll be there in the fall is what you need," Riskin shook his head.

"Why, where you going?"

"What happened to your last one?" Riskin inquired. "I thought they never left Dexter."

"Answer my question."

"I won't be around. Now answer mine."

"He shot himself in the foot: Beer I can stand, but you don't do dope in Dexter--not on my coaching staff. So where you going?"

"If I knew that, I'd probably be on my way there already," Riskin shrugged.

"Then you might still be here in September?" Holt persisted.

Riskin took a long gulp of beer. "No way," he said. "Besides, I was a flanker. My coach was saving me for basketball."

"I'll make my receiver coach my halfback coach," Holt started plotting. "Kelly was an all-purpose back anyway when he played for me."

"Then pay him double and make him an all-purpose coach."

UNDER FRIENDLY FIRE

"When I've got a receiver coach like you available."

"I'm *not* available," Riskin insisted. "Besides, I only caught twelve passes in three years. We were a 'three yards and a cloud of dust' team."

"Well, we're a wide-open pro-set kind of team," Holt bragged and waved for two more from the tender.

"I'm not even finished with my first one," Riskin held his bottle up.

"Then whatta you waiting for," Holt carried on. "I'll have Floyd bring us a contract, too."

"Coach, I can tell you right now, I never sign anything important when I'm drinking one or two beers; I've got to be stone drunk like I was when I enlisted in the Army," Riskin grinned.

"Well, Floyd can fix that, too," Holt came back.

"Jim," the voice said from behind him. He could not place it until he swiveled in his stool. Then he could place it but he could not believe it. "Can I talk to you--alone?"

The face, the figure in a tight calico dress said it was Breezy McLachin. The tone said it was somebody else he did not know, had never met before. She motioned toward a table on the other side of the dance floor, was already on her way over there before he said anything.

"Careful." This time he distinctly heard Holt say it.

MICHAEL CORNELL

The band was back, broke into *Wake Up Little Susie*. Breezy was still standing when he walked over. "Let's go outside," she called out above the music. Riskin followed like before, just like who-knows-how-many other fools before him, he thought. So much for hard-to-get.

They were sitting in her pickup truck. The windows were rolled up against the chilly night air, unseasonable for this time of year. He spoke first: "Do something for me: Don't set me up this time, all right? And see me back to my Jeep, okay?"

"I'm sorry about the other day," Breezy said, looking straight at him.

"It was yesterday," he corrected her.

"Then we can start over today?"

"Did we start something yesterday?"

"I don't know, did we?"

Riskin wanted to look away, felt as though a light were trained upon him. She would not let him. She leaned over, he was watching her the whole time, but he did not see her do it. She kissed him, felt her lips pressed against his, her mouth open, his eyes closed. One moment he was clutching a handful of calico; the next, as the image of her stripping atop a table for a cheering, drunken mob flashed before him, he was wanting to pull away. The only one doing the releasing was Breezy McLachin.

UNDER FRIENDLY FIRE

"I was wrong." she was whispering to him and for the first time he caught the true color of her blue-green eyes in the reflected light of the parking lot. "You wanted to talk to me, tell me something, and I wouldn't let you."

Now Riskin was doing the withdrawing. Suddenly she had made him remember, as suddenly as she had made him forget. He leaned his back against the passenger side-door. The armrest dug uncomfortably into his spine as the memory of a few months before insinuated itself painfully into his consciousness. The words came more easily than he ever thought they could.

"I killed Zed." Not her husband. Not Zachary McLachin. Zed. As though he knew him, had always known him.

Her expression did not change. Only the eyes seemed to change. Somehow the blue had seemed to drain from them, the green now dominating, now taking over completely. Riskin was certain he had imagined it.

The words that followed the words came much more haltingly, more lagging in their flow. It was the description of the incident itself, the same one he had gone over time and again: the kind of night it was, how the sand was swirling fiercely, how the pilot and crew lost even their most rudimentary powers of navigation, how the black blur of the all-terrain vehicle was spotted, how the order was given.

How *he* squeezed the trigger.

She still sat motionless, her face the same, expressionless. He could have just recounted the conclusion of a movie to her, instead of the conclusion of her life as she had known it with Zed. It made him want desperately to know what she was thinking but he was too terrified to ask. He only knew that the circumstances he had related, the darkness, the sand, even the errant order were the flimsiest of straws, that he, Jimmy Riskin, had *murdered* Zed as surely as though it had been the most premeditated of homicides.

He reached for the handle, left the truck. Now *he* was doing the walking. Now *he* was praying some car would come careening into the gravel parking lane and smack him dead.

Riskin could not remember the last time one of his prayers was answered.

Chapter 10

Destinies

UNDER FRIENDLY FIRE

TEN

"You been cryin'," Ginny Walker said as she opened the door. Breezy could see the gentle warmth of the candlelight. "Why you been cryin'?"

"I haven't been," she lied, stepping inside.

"No good lyin' to me," the old black woman shook her head. "Lyin' could get you a spankin', but you'd probably enjoy it too much. Now what's it this time as if I didn't know?"

"It's him all right, Ginny," Breezy admitted, sitting down at the slanting card table without waiting to be asked, "but something cruel has entered into it."

"Cruel like fate, huh?" Ginny nodded as she went to the cupboard, brought back some fruit juice and sat.

Breezy took a sip of hers.

"What-say you tell me," the old woman offered, "and let *me* be the judge of how cruel fate's been to you."

Breezy related the nature, then detailed circumstances of Jim Riskin's revelation to her. It came easier than she thought it would, nearly as easy as the juice went down.

"Seems to me, there's another way of lookin' at this thing," Ginny smiled a thin, knowing smile, "and that's maybe the terrible thing that happened was a destiny of another sort. You forget, you never told me anything about this Riskin fella 'cause I never asked you to; now you're tellin' me what he told you like he was somebody you been knowin' a long time-- and want to be knowin' a long time more."

Breezy looked away uneasily at the green Coke bottles stirring with a quiet tinkling noise in the open windows.

"Well, at least you listened to the last thing I told you," Ginny chuckled.

Breezy looked over again.

"'Bout lettin' him stay put in your brain and not tryin' to lock him out," the old woman observed. "That means there's still somethin' behind them pretty yellow curls of yours."

Now Breezy smiled. "Ginny," she said shyly and stopped.

"Sure," the elderly lady grinned and motioned toward the old Army cot. "You get your things off and I'll mix the rubbin' solution."

UNDER FRIENDLY FIRE

In minutes, she was drifting off again, as she always did at Ginny Walker's, far, far away. Once more, she felt the busy fingers traveling everywhere they pleased, anywhere she pleased. Again, she could hear the distant, playful spanking of a baby's bare butt; again, she could feel the smooth milkiness of Ginny's rubbing concoction.

At her wettest, as she seemed to be drowning in the juices of her own dreamy ecstacy, she was kissing Jim Riskin full on the mouth and his long sure fingers were on their own expeditionary jaunt. Superimposed over it all, as on a television screen, were what appeared to be transparent building blocks spelling out the letters J-I-M.

The warm, healing waters of Ginny's large metal tub followed, and after, she was seated once again in her white nakedness at the table. This time the small burlap pouch was nowhere to be seen, only the quiet light of the dripping candle.

"Don't fight it, girl," the old woman was telling her in her canny, assertive way. "Zed's gone but Breezy is very much alive, but only if you let her live and explore and strive to be the person she is."

It was difficult for Breezy to fathom that this was the same person who, by her own admission, had only known three years of formal education, who had virtually lived off the land for her entire eighty-some years, who had outlived four husbands and countless other men, all, Breezy was certain, could not hold a candle to her intelligence *or* wisdom. Neither the brains nor the understanding amazed, but the eloquence of expression. Live and explore and strive.

"And the beautiful thing about it," Ginny Walker continued, "is that *he* feels the same way about you."

"How can you know *that?*" Breezy asked just to be saying something.

"'Cause that's what makes it so confusing, so frustrating," she answered. "You been through some things, first with your folks dyin' in the accident, now with Zed goin' like he did in the war, and you just can't believe somethin' good could be happenin' to Breezy McLachin. You're sayin' it's got to be some kinda mistake of providence or whatever you want to call it, so you're willin' to flat-out ignore the whole thing or try to sweep it away like it never happened to you. I done it myself, *me*, with more old men and lovers than you could shake a fist at."

She stopped, then started again, more slowly: "It happened a long, long time ago, after my first husband died and I was wishin' my second one would follow. I passed on somebody that I will know 'til my dyin' day that I shoulda never passed on, somethin' that has haunted me, eaten away at me ever since. He was a soldier, too, like Zed was and this Jim Riskin was. His name was Coley, Coley Burrell. He wasn't much to look at maybe, not like some of the other men I had, but he was the most carin' man I ever known and, more important than that, he was the right man for me. It's somethin' I just knew, but was too damn scared to do nothin' about."

"What happened to him?" Breezy wanted to know though hesitant about breaking the reverie.

"He died in the Second War," the old woman replied, "and I died with him, 'cause I never told him what he was to me. I let him go off without saying even half as much as I shoulda said, like he was some kind of mind reader or somethin'. Well, men might be good for a lotta things women want, good men, but they ain't much good for readin' womens' minds."

Ginny Walker paused once more, then said: "Don't let Jim Riskin be your Coley Burrell."

Chapter 11

Fallon's Point

UNDER FRIENDLY FIRE

ELEVEN

On the telephone the request had a strange sound to it. A week later when the Jaguar's parts arrived and the car was dropped by for their installation, Mrs. Fallon asked that Riskin deliver it to her at Fallon's Point, a heavily wooded spot that represented the highest point of elevation in the area and that he himself must have passed on the way up to Dexter.

When she came into view standing next to her minivan, the request had all the logic in the world. She was dressed in a yellow-pastel jumpsuit that fastened like bib overalls on top but tighter, and was cut short like trouble on the bottom. On her small feet were Betty Grable-like high heels of a matching yellow with straps that tied around her slim ankles, hardly the regulation footwear for trekking through the woods. Riskin was not complaining. In the outfit, Mrs. Fallon could have been twenty-two or not a month older than twenty-six, a physical impossibility since her son

MICHAEL CORNELL

Brandon was eleven or twelve and she would have been enrolled in an exclusive convent school at the chronological age in question. Riskin was still not complaining.

"Did you have any trouble finding it?" she asked as he drove up in the Jag, top down.

"Nope," he grinned a stupid grin. "I spotted your yellow outfit a long way back--in a dream when I was about thirteen years old."

"And do you still have dreams like that?"

"All the time, but I prefer to be awake now when I have 'em." His own subtlety was starting to amaze him. He really had been Stateside a month now, he marveled; either that, or Dexter was growing on him. He hoped to hell it was the former.

"You know, you could be shot coming up here to meet me like this," she suddenly informed him.

"I could have been shot in the frigging desert," he returned, looking over the expanse of rolling green. "This place is prettier."

"It gets prettier," she promised, walking ahead.

Riskin followed.

"What are you going to do with yourself now that you're out?" she inquired, letting him catch up but still leading.

"Ask me in about a month," he said.

"What happens in a month?"

UNDER FRIENDLY FIRE

"That depends," he thought it over, "but if nothing happens then maybe I should be back in Army duds. Between me and my father, that's all I've known."

"Don't you think a statement like that is an admission of defeat?" she remarked as they neared a fallen tree. The way it was broken at the stump it looked as though lightening had struck it. Or a pickup truck.

"Maybe it is," he nodded. "Or maybe it's an admission of my limitations. I had a good friend in the service, a guy named Levine from New York City, who tried to teach me some art and music and that kind of cultural stuff."

She sat down on the dead tree trunk. He sat next to her, resumed: "Well, he failed miserably at that. But what he did leave me with was this: Limitations. Levine was always talking about knowing your limitations. He used to say it didn't matter if you had the greatest plans and schemes in the world, but if they weren't attainable, they weren't too great at all. He said he was going to write a book someday and call it: *Reachable Dreams*. I told him it would be a best-seller, because even if nobody else bought it, I'd buy up all the copies. Kind of like that song *Nashville Cats*: 'Nobody will buy my record, but *I* will.'"

Sitting next to him but out of nowhere she asked: "Can I kiss you?"

Riskin looked at her, said: "Why would you want to do that?"

"Does a woman have to have a reason? Do you think I'm trying to get you shot or something?"

"No, but maybe you're trying to get *you* shot?" He leaned back as far as he could. "You're not too happy, are you, Mrs. Fallon?"

"What if I told you that that's something I gave up on a long time ago?" she wanted to know.

"I'd say you're making yourself sound a whole lot older than you are." He was sorry he said it as soon as it came out, tried to reverse his field: "Besides, what is it about Dexter that the women always seem to be making the first move."

Mrs. Fallon laughed her trained, cultured laugh.

"Why, how many women have tried to kiss you since you arrived in Dexter?" she inquired with the same directness. "I mean, besides Breezy McLachin."

Riskin looked away.

"That's okay," she pressed on, "I kind of deduced it was Dexter's official war widow you'd come to see and, naturally, she'd come to see you. She usually does, or so goes general consensus around here. Breezy's sort of what you would call Dexter's own personal welcome wagon or so I am told."

"And do you believe everything you're told?" He was looking back at her and for the first time he detected tiny lines around her eyes. Somehow it made her look even more beautiful.

"When you hear something enough times--"

"When you hear something enough times," he cut her off, "it generally means a lot of people resent you or what you stand for."

"Oh, now Breezy *stands* for something," she was taken aback.

"Who stands for anything nowadays," he reacted. "Why does anybody have to stand for any damn thing anyway. Why can't people just let you be one of them?"

"You're asking the wrong person," she shot back. "A Fallon has never been 'one of them' around here. Do you think all those idiots in the stands were pulling for you to yank my Brandon last week for a pinch-hitter because he was just 'one of them'?"

"*I* think they wanted me to yank him because *they* thought he wouldn't get a hit," he stated flat-out.

"Neither did I," she abruptly broke into a laugh, not trained, not cultured.

"I don't even know your first name," he smiled warmly, the tension broken.

"Whitney."

"Whitney, can I kiss you?" he asked with all the formality he could manage to fake.

"Aren't you afraid it might get you shot?"

"You keep saying that," he leaned close to her.

MICHAEL CORNELL

He did not let her finish what she was saying. She could not. Riskin wondered if Mayor Fallon and the rest of the small-town mayors were drooling over some busty stripping telegram out of an oversized cupcake at that precise moment. As he kissed her, he did not care about cupcakes *or*, for that matter, small-town mayors.

"There's a little spring close by I like to escape to by myself," she intimated, her voice low and refined once more, but with the pleasant tone of a shared confidence.

Following was something he was getting better and better at, he thought to himself.

On the soft grass by the spring, it was the first time he had been naked with a woman since before the Gulf. And the last one was nothing like Mrs. Fallon. Whitney.

There were three, four times he could have easily gone off, but he held himself to savor the moment, his freedom and, most of all, his partner. Her beauty, the flawless, scented skin of her body, held its own in the stark daylight, was not the least deterred. More than anything, he wanted desperately to satisfy *her*, more than he was willing to satisfy himself.

When it was over, even immediately after withdrawal, he was certain of one thing: Mayor Fallon was a bigger idiot than any of those people at the Little League game.

UNDER FRIENDLY FIRE

If not, what in the world was he doing watching some cheap stripper in a cheaper G-string at the cheapest convention of small-town mayors in God-knows-where when there was a spring like the one at Fallon's Point.

Chapter 12

Velvet

UNDER FRIENDLY FIRE

TWELVE

Other than the one-punch decision he scored over Breezy's attacker the first night, the first real fight Jimmy Riskin got into in Dexter--if three against one constituted a fight--did not involve large truckers with cut-off denim sleeves. All three were dressed in business suits but with the working pair looking more like poormen's Memphis Mafia than CPA's. Tim Holt prevented the confrontation from being more. He had also precipitated the venue.

Riskin had stood by silently when Holt introduced him at the first summer football workout as the Zephers' new receiver coach. A light touch drill of pass and catch demonstrated enough promise to warrant pre-season optimism, understandable on a team with thirteen returning lettermen, and Riskin found himself getting caught up in the high school camaraderie generated by the veteran coach. After the workout, on a dare from Holt he could not refuse, he

MICHAEL CORNELL

engaged some of the varsity basketball players from the football squad in rotating games of one-on-one in the school gym. After working the rust out and gaining his wind, Riskin proceeded to put on a hardcourt clinic to the wonderment of his younger opponents. Whether driving or popping all-netters from three-point range, Riskin exhibited the kind of all-around speed and versatility generally associated with black hoopsters. Nobody was more impressed than Tim Holt, no one less impressed than Riskin himself. Basketball had always been his sport and always would be--even if the last other *white* player in the world was some seven-foot-five Yugoslavian with big hands and slow feet.

When he emerged from the locker room after his shower, they confronted him. The first one, who could have been Dexter's youngest-ever bank president, did all the talking: "Stay away from Fallon's Point," was all he said in a low, modulated tone that made it sound as though he had rehearsed the five words five hundred times to get the right, measured sound.

Then, one of his stooges launched into an embarrassing foot-first leap that looked like a how-not-to move from a mail-order kung-fu course. The kick glanced harmlessly off Riskin's side and the goon in the gray flannel suit crashed on *his* side on the hard gym floor. The other flunky tried to land a round-house from too far back and Riskin, now poised for

UNDER FRIENDLY FIRE

anything, easily countered with a solid right to the man's cheekbone that landed him free-fall on top of his buddy. Larry and Moe could have done it better without Curley's help at all. At this point, Holt entered the gym, shot the spokesman a look without saying a word, and watched the three of them leave.

"What did Powers want?" Holt asked when the gym door slammed shut.

"Who's Powers?"

"The cool one in the suit that fits," the coach answered. "He's the Mayor's brother-in-law, step-brother of Whitney Fallon. He runs a trucking business. What'd he want?"

"He wanted me to stay away from Fallon's Point."

"Why would it take him two of his huskies to tell you that?" Holt continued his grilling.

"I thought maybe Fallon's Point was one of the branch offices or something."

Holt shook his head, said: "Riskin, you're a helluva basketball player and you might make a helluva receiver coach, but you're a real smart ass, you know that? Let's hit the diner for something to eat."

"The diner?" Riskin raised the flag. Breezy was probably working there today.

"Yeah, what's wrong with the diner?"

"Don't you remember what you told me?" Riskin queried him now.

Holt furrowed his brow.

"You said 'careful'," Riskin reminded him.

Holt broke into a grin. "Since when did you ever listen to anything the old coach told you," he said as though the two had known each other for considerably more than a week and a half.

They headed off together.

Breezy was working. They sat in the same booth he had waited for her last time, the one by the door, with Riskin looking in. He wanted to study her, get her out of his system and, fueled by the image of Whitney Fallon whom he had met twice more at the Point, he was convinced he could do it.

Whitney had it all over Breezy, he said to himself. She had intelligence to complement her beauty, a finishing school class that Breezy would never possess. That she had a rich, powerful husband as well was testament to her own considerable powers of feminine completeness. Whitney had all those things and he had Whitney for now. For now was good enough, he thought.

Breezy came over, said hello to neither in particular, took their order. Riskin watched her return to the pickup window. Her walk had a weariness to it that he had not noticed before; even the audible cling of her thin waitress outfit to her slip was missing when she moved. For some reason, he resented it and in his mind began dressing her--that was a funny thing to be

UNDER FRIENDLY FIRE

doing, he smiled to himself--in light, airy things like the calico dress she had worn the other night, or the pastel-yellow jumpsuit Whitney had worn the first time at Fallon Point. Whitney Fallon. Breezy McLachin could probably hang every damn stitch she had in the darkest corner of *Mrs.* Fallon's wardrobe.

Breezy returned with their order.

"Don't go," he said, almost reaching out to grab her, completely oblivious of Coach Holt.

She stopped, her mouth slightly open, her blue-green eyes wide open. He plowed on: "Listen, if you're not doing anything tonight, I'd love to take you to dinner," he offered with the openness of a school boy, "preferably someplace outside of Dexter."

Holt was as disarmed as she was. All he could do was watch. All she could do was tell him to go to hell. She said: "Should I wear something kind of formal?"

"Hell, no." he kept going, "you should wear something brand new. Where's the nearest monster-mall like they got in normal American cities?"

"Somerset's the other side of the Interstate," Holt volunteered. "It'll be opened 'til nine."

"I'll be ready at six," she smiled and he wanted to toss his damn hamburger up against the restaurant wall; he was not hungry anymore, not in the damn least.

"Like I said," the coach grinned and took a bite of his, "you Riskin are a real smart ass." His mouth was

MICHAEL CORNELL

full of ground round when he said it but Riskin did not hear him anyway.

Breezy McLachin had it all over Whitney Fallon. The quiet candlelight played off the smooth white skin of her shoulders, the blue-velvet sheen of her crinkly new, low-cut evening dress, the end result of his entire first week's pay from Flaherty. Riskin did not care. Breezy looked good enough to eat, better.
"You *do* know you could have your way with me tonight just about any way you pleased," she was saying.
Riskin laughed, leaned forward: "No, I couldn't."
She looked at him quizzically. Her eyes were pure-blue now. He explained: "I feel like I did on my prom night--and I didn't even go to my prom."
"*That* I find hard to believe," she observed, her blue eyes dancing from his thick, sandy-brown hair to his neat brown suit and back.
"It's true," he recounted, "the girl I wanted to take got asked by someone else first."
"The story of every girl's life," Breezy threw her head back philosophically. Whitney Fallon could not have done it better.
"So I didn't go," he resumed. "And tonight, looking at you, I feel the same way I did then. You're so beautiful, I probably wouldn't be a damn bit of good tonight. I'd probably go limper than an airport

UNDER FRIENDLY FIRE

wind sock on a muggy day, just thinking about you and trying too hard."

"Man doesn't got to do all the tryin', you know," she smiled.

Chapter 13

Break Point

THIRTEEN

Riskin was not much good the next day at Flaherty's station. The sex with Breezy had been the most physically exhausting of his life; it had also been the most physically satisfying he had ever experienced. His anxieties about his own ability to perform had been totally unfounded with each lover contributing equally in a passionate sharing, a mutual caring for one another's carnal needs. The solitary drawback for Riskin was the personal guilt it imparted upon him for the time he had spent with Whitney. For someone else who had been isolated as he had been isolated in the Gulf, it may have been ego-salving to have known two women as desirable as Breezy and Whitney in the shortest of time spans. For Riskin, it only had the effect of making him feel cheap; worse, it made him mercenary and dirty. He resolved to end whatever it was that he started with Whitney Fallon as soon as he was able.

MICHAEL CORNELL

Soon came faster than he had anticipated when the red Jaguar roadster pulled up to the service bay in the late afternoon. It was idling nicely since he fixed it.

"Your brother dropped by to see me," he said. It was a suitable opening for what he had to tell her.

"That's just it: Ricky Lee's *not* my brother," she answered coolly. "He's my stepbrother and he's never let me forget it."

"Okay, stepbrother then, but he brought two of his business associates with him when he dropped by."

"That's so he wouldn't have to wrinkle his own new suit." Now she was being matter-of-fact and it bothered him. "What'd you tell him?"

"It's not what I told *him*," Riskin replied, "It's what he might tell your husband."

"Ricky Lee won't tell him a *damn* thing." It was the first time he had heard her use the word or any word like it. "Ricky Lee's too jealous of my husband. Being my stepbrother was like the great curse of his spoiled, self-centered life. The way it was wouldn't even have qualified as good, clean incest."

Riskin looked up to see Breezy McLachin approaching from the direction of the diner.

"You got some time?" Whitney brightened up, unaware of his new concern.

"Time?" he repeated stupidly.

"Yes. It's what they sell watches for," she kidded. "Otherwise, people wouldn't have any time to *do* anything. All we'd need is a little thirty minutes of it up at the Point."

"Sure," Riskin accepted hurriedly, just to get rid of her. "I get off in twenty minutes."

"I know when you get off," Whitney smiled, then turned her head at the sound of Breezy's footsteps.

They stopped. The two women looked at each other, did not say anything.

"See you in a little, Jimmy," Whitney faced him again, threw the Jag into gear, drove off.

"*Jimmy*," Breezy laughed a little hurt laugh, then turned to retrace her steps. He wanted to run after her but he did not know what to say to her. He was too damn dumb. It was the one thing he was absolutely certain of.

Dumb got dumber, Riskin thought, as he pulled up to the Point forty-five minutes later. He could see Whitney's red convertible parked a ways into the woods. He could also see the silver Mercedes drive up from the other direction. The windows were black but even someone as half-baked as he felt would know who its passengers were, all three of them.

The best punches were Riskin's; there just were not enough of them, no more than one for every two of theirs before he lost count. But it was the kick that did him in, from the blind side, as he lay on the ground, compliments of Ricky Lee Powers. Riskin was sure it must have re-creased the sonofabitch's pants, because it put what felt like a new rung where there had not been one before on the right side of *his* rib cage.

Whitney had tried to stop it, but the best she could do was a feeble attempt to comfort him after kin and friends were gone. His response was equally feeble, sputtering incoherently about the damage looking worse than it was or something nearly as inane. He told her to get the hell off the Point, that he would be all right as soon a he caught his wind. Somehow it worked.

It was a good hour after she left that he managed to start up the Jeep and point it in the direction of the friendly city limits of Dexter.

In the worst way he wanted to see Breezy McLachin, to be with her, but the prospects were getting as dim as the two-laner.

She was lying down, still in her waitress uniform and hosiery, when she heard the knock. She hoped it was him, though its tentativeness did not sound the way he would knock. Going to the door, she cracked it open.

In a split second he was inside, the large guy who had attacked her in her truck the night she first met Jim Riskin. The bastard had a patch of electrical tape over her mouth before she could cry out and was dragging her across the living room.

UNDER FRIENDLY FIRE

"Now maybe you'll finish that little striptease you started at The Hopper a week or so ago," he was laughing through clenched teeth, his breath reeking of hard liquor.

Breezy fought back with all the adrenalin her suddenly shocked state could muster, but the man's strength was impossible to overcome in spite of the alcohol he had consumed. In moments she was flat on her back across her bed and he was ripping away the flimsy material of her uniform. As he fumbled anxiously with her slip, she tried to poke him in the eyes with her fingernails, missed, but somehow elbowed him hard on the wide bridge of his nose. Suddenly, blood was gushing forth as from a broken faucet, over his animal-face, his open shirt, and her own white slip.

"Damn you!" he let out a clenched howl in a much higher tone than his hulking build would seem to be capable and a flash-recollection of Riskin landing a punch that first night to the same spot, his fat nose, moved her to repeat her original unwitting blow.

The second elbow had him clutching his face in serious agony and allowed her to slip her small frame from under his suffocating bulk. In a second more, she had the tape off and Zed's military revolver out of the night table and aimed straight at his bleeding, ugly snout.

MICHAEL CORNELL

She said with a calm that belonged to someone else: "Get the hell out of here or I'll blow your brains all over these damn walls."

One, two ribs could have been broken the way they felt. Riskin lay on his bed feeling his side, wanting to call her, but wanting to *see* her more. The pain, the drowsiness relieving it, told him he was going nowhere and staying at the Rustic this night. There were worse places but he could not remember where in America they were.

Chapter 14

Notions

UNDER FRIENDLY FIRE

FOURTEEN

In the morning it was all Breezy McLachin could do to try to gather herself, shower, and remove any telltale reminders of the sonofabitch's blood from the bedspread and the carpet of her trailer. Her bloodstained slip she would burn. All she knew was that her entire being seemed drained of combatant energy. Thirty-six hours ago, Jimmy Riskin had made her feel prettier, more beautiful than she had ever been made to feel.

Somehow she managed to trudge wearily to her narrow wardrobe, take out a clean uniform and start to dress, only to head off once more to the shower and its sterilizing rush of hot water. It was five of seven when she finally stood before the bedroom mirror in a fresh new waitress outfit.

Working would make her forget; staying put would make her remember and, since Zed had been killed, there was much more to forget than to remember.

When she arrived at the Diner, no one was there at the counter or in any of the booths. Only Ted Bolan manning his usual station in the kitchen and waiting for business to commence. Breezy walked up to him, put her arms around him, smothered her face in his clean apron. She was crying but tears were not coming out. Everything else felt the same.

"There, there," he comforted her, "new day, this one's gonna be a whole lot better."

She wanted to believe him. She had to.

"But listen to an old dog's advice," the soft, burly man continued, "maybe you should try staying home some nights."

I did, she wanted to say, but somebody dropped by. She did not say anything.

"You'll be all right," Ted patted her back, "starting now, round one: we got a customer."

Breezy broke the embrace, wiped her eyes. They were still dry. She took out her order pad, walked over.

"Good morning, *Jimmy*," she greeted him with Whitney's word.

"That's my name all right," he said, before predictably adding: "Listen Breezy, it's not how it looks between Whitney Fallon and me."

"You tell me how it looks then, soldier."

UNDER FRIENDLY FIRE

"Don't call me *that* again," he snapped. "I'm not a soldier anymore, and I'm not going to be, if I can help it."

"That's your problem to work out," she returned.

"*You're* my problem," he told her, looking straight into her green eyes.

"I'm nobody's problem but my own," she asserted. "But tell me about Whitney anyway."

"She's a married woman." It sounded trite and stupid and Riskin knew it. He tried to return some semblance of credibility to the response: "I thought there might be something there; I was wrong."

"And with us?"

"I'm not wrong."

"Well, maybe you want to test the waters a little more to make sure." She was sorry she said it as soon as she did. Thank God he could tell.

He smiled: "Number six," he said pointing to the menu board.

"There isn't no number six."

"I know. It's for hamburgers and a movie show tonight."

Breezy wanted to cry again, but this time the tears would have shown. It was just good enough for her to know that she would live after all, after last night.

The movie was awful, but the most disconcerting part about it was that they seemed to be the only ones in the Somerset complex theater who thought so. The rest of the audience, mostly of high school age, celebrated it as though the film marked the return of Hitchcock. To compound matters, the storyline in all its grisly glory centered upon a psychopathic serial rapist, the last thing Breezy needed after the attack of the night before. She and Riskin left before the psycho was apprehended by the nearly unsympathetic, misogynistic police inspector.

On a whim, Breezy suggested they drop into "Pop" Daniels' Bar when they returned to Dexter. Daniels had been the long-time Dexter High sports coach before Tim Holt. At sixty-seven, he still seemed to be going strong--even if his bar was not--and loved waxing dramatic about all things athletic. Riskin hit it off with him at once.

"Sure, I hearda you, Riskin," Pop claimed dogmatically. "Aren't too many white basketball players left and you were one of the best of that year's high school crop."

Riskin only half-believed him though he *had* been selected to the second squad on *Parade* Magazine's High School All-American Team. It really did not matter. He liked Daniels and he liked his cozy bar. Like the movie earlier, however, neither he nor Breezy seemed to be on the popular side of consensus. There was no one else in the place but the three of them and Pop did not count because he was the owner.

UNDER FRIENDLY FIRE

"Is this a normal night in here?" Riskin finally asked him when he was able to take a time-out from the sports talk.

"What's normal?" the old former coach laughed wryly. "If you mean is this like it is every Friday night, well, no it isn't. Last Friday I had five customers in here--not five at once, mind you--but five was the official attendance. But why don't you ask me about last night, Thursday night?"

Riskin did not have to.

"I closed up at nine," Pop told him anyway.

"I don't figure it," Riskin shook his head. "I haven't been in Dexter that long, but I've been here long enough to know that people here love their sports."

He looked around the room at the vast collection of trophies, jerseys and sundry sports memorabilia, looked back at Daniels: "It doesn't figure," he said again. "Hadn't been for Breezy, I wouldn't even have known about your place."

"That's because Breezy and Zed used to be part of the regulars," Pop enlightened him, but in a tone that seemed to be in quiet deference to Zed McLachin's memory, something that did not score well with Breezy. Heroic death was one thing, but Zed was hardly ready for canonization.

"Listen, Pop, I appreciate the respect and all that," she let him know, "but it's not going to hurt me none to talk about Zed or about us coming to your place as much as we did."

"Then how come you stayed away so long to come back?" Daniels countered, but in the same sympathetic tone.

"Because until I met Jim--"

"Jimmy," Riskin interjected.

She looked across at him, smiled and almost lost her thought. "Because until I met Jimmy," she recovered, "I had no reason to come back here again. Now I got the feeling I'm--we're--going to be coming back a lot."

"Well, if you could start bringing the camp followers you and Zed had back in here, I might even consider staying open a while longer," Pop remarked.

Breezy seemed stunned; Riskin was just surprised.

"You're thinking of closing?" she asked in disbelief.

"You got the *only* sports bar in Dexter and you're going to pick up stakes?" Riskin followed: Pop Daniels seemed too embarrassed to answer either.

"I'll tell you something, Pop," Riskin went on, "you're missing a real bet if you do. Didn't you ever think of putting up a satellite dish and showing pro and college games on a big screen every night?"

"Sure, I thought of it, but the damn things are outlawed in Dexter, just like cable," Daniels informed

UNDER FRIENDLY FIRE

him, "and you can thank the Honorable Rance Fallon for that."

"Mayor Fallon?" Riskin inquired.

"The same one," Daniels continued. "Seems he's convinced the town council that cable television and satellite dishes would corrupt the homespun charm of our little burg. It'll also steal business from his baby *The Big Hopper.*

"Fallon owns The Hopper?"

Pop's head bobbed up and down and for the first time Riskin noticed that the eye next to the wall was glass. It was a good likeness and everything else about the man's open, ruddy face was genuine.

"I know cable franchises are political footballs," Riskin observed, "but I'd be willing to test the legality of somebody blocking you from buying your own dish if I were you, Pop."

"So I get a sharp outtatown lawyer to help me get a dish," the old coach started thinking out loud, "but who's going to pay to pave that rutty, dirt road leading up to my place? Why, when it rains, you'd think it was Johnstown Revisited."

He added: "and I swear Fallon has his boys soak it down when it doesn't rain."

Breezy finally spoke: "Pop, what if somebody could get you some money to pave the road and buy the satellite dish and turn this place of yours around--"

"I'd kiss him on the melon," Daniels put her off with a laugh.

"Yeah, but would you take 'em as a partner?" Breezy resumed her line of reasoning.

"Well, it depends who the partner was," he said. "But where are you going to find a fool that big--even in a town this small?"

"*I'm* going to be receiving a life insurance settlement," she divulged, "for Zed's death."

Riskin was taken aback; he listened anyway. So did Pop Daniels, but only to a point: "You'd be wasting your money," he interrupted her cursory explanation of the settlement's terms. "Not only that, but you'd be desecrating the memory of your husband."

"That's pure crap," Breezy objected. "Zed loved this place. He would've been proud to have a piece of it."

Riskin, who had been fighting the notion that he himself had authored the policy's pay-off clause, stepped in: "Listen, Pop, what if the money came from somewhere else, or from a group of partners who each had a piece," he angled. "What if the money came from Breezy, from me, from, say, somebody else like Tim Holt."

"Tim Holt and me don't talk anymore," Daniels stated with unbending firmness. "He never even invites

UNDER FRIENDLY FIRE

me to make a guest appearance at the high school athletic banquet. Afraid that I might upstage him."

"I find that a little hard to believe," Riskin smirked.

"Well, you can believe it anyway," Daniels insisted. "The shame of it is that he's been socking the paychecks away for years. The man doesn't got any family. His boys on the football and basketball squads are all he has."

"And is that so bad?" Riskin straightened the smirk.

"No, I guess not, but he doesn't have to spend what little he does spend at Fallon's Hopper."

"Maybe he wouldn't if he had a reason to go someplace else, Pop," Breezy threw her change in.

Riskin regarded her as she did. Her eyes were pure blue again.

"Tell me about you two," Daniels suddenly changed the subject and Riskin knew he must have been watching him watching her.

Breezy did not know how to respond but she liked the sound of the question. "I haven't met Jimmy before" was all she could manage.

Chapter 15

Belongings

UNDER FRIENDLY FIRE

FIFTEEN

The trick play was probably the oldest trick play in the book. It was the perfection of execution and the juncture it was called, with thirty-six seconds left in the Dexter High School blue-white scrimmage, that made Riskin an instant hero in Tim Holt's eyes again. The football was snapped directly to the blocking back and, while the receivers flooded the left sideline and took the defensive backs with them, the quarterback streaked down the right hashmark, caught the pass without breaking stride and dashed forty-seven yards to give Riskin's blue squad the victory over the backfield coach's white team. Both assistants had fared well on head coach Holt's clipboard checklist but this time Riskin had come out on the top end of the score.

There was another kind of magic to the moment, Riskin thought, as he waved to Breezy high in the stands under the glare of the field's lights. It was the magic of belonging to someplace with everybody there watching, but mostly of *her* watching and cheering him on as fervently as she ever could have cheered on Zed McLachin.

"Don't matter if it's baseball or football," Holt was slapping him on the back, "you just keep pulling 'em out and pulling 'em off. Well, smart ass, where do I treat you this time, the Somerset Steak Wagon?"

Riskin seized the opening: "Nope, Pop Daniel's Bar."

Holt went nearly as rigid as Daniels had. "Aw come on, you can do better than that," he tried to joke.

"No, I can't," Riskin asserted, "and neither can the team if Pop just serves them soda pop like his name implies."

Holt was really having a difficult time of it, Riskin could see, but he finally folded: "All right, winners get their way," he said.

"What gives with you two anyway?" Riskin just had to ask.

"Nothing with me," He attempted to pass it off, "but the old man still thinks I'm playing for him, which means he still wants to call the plays. Well, there's one head coach at Dexter and Holt's his name, I'm not sorry to say."

"When was the last time you two talked?"

"Ask *him, I can't remember.*"

UNDER FRIENDLY FIRE

"Well, for what it's worth, I think Pop's got the picture about who's coach and who's not," Riskin finished his bit. "Mind if I bring Breezy?"

"I'd mind more if I had to stare at your mug the rest of the night," Holt slapped him again and went to round up the players.

The team visit, and particularly the appearancce of Holt, knocked the sweat socks off the old man. But Holt had a surprise of his own for Riskin: a check from Dexter High's accounting office in *his* name.

"What's this?" Riskin was dumbstruck and he saw no reason for hiding it.

"I know it's not much," Holt returned appreciatively, "but it's compensation to my new receiver coach, official-like."

Riskin looked at Breezy who intuitively seemed to be sensing the same feeling of belonging for him that he was sensing, then back at Holt, but he was too choked up to say anything. It was a new experience for him, so new he did not know how to react. Even when he was winning basketball games for his old high school team with his jumpshots, he never felt like he belonged because of the transient nature of his military family's existence.

"Nice to shut you up for a change, Riskin," Holt kidded him. "Now tell me the *real* reason you brought me here. Just forget about me kissing Pop on his grizzled butt and us making up, that's all."

129

MICHAEL CORNELL

"My butt ain't grizzled, Holt," Pop Daniels cut in from out of the blue with free rounds for their table. "But if you want to shake hands and invite me to your damned athletic banquet this winter, I promise not to speak more than an hour."

Holt stared at his old coach for what seemed like a half a minute, then answered the bell. "So you promise to cut it short this year, huh?"

"Well, if you'd dream up some imaginative plays this year, I wouldn't have to talk so long about the glory days," Pop came back.

"Hell, when you had players like me, it was easy for you to be copping the glory."

"Hell, the only thing you ever gave your old coach credit for, Holt, was your foot-speed--and you didn't have none."

The two went at each other like that for another six rounds of verbal sparring before Riskin spoiled their fun by laughing too hard and breaking their rhythm.

"Okay, what's so funny, smart ass?" Holt asked what both he and Daniels wanted to know.

"Well, you're right, Coach," he started, trying to wipe the stupid grin off his face, "I did bring you here to have you two kiss and make up. The trouble is, you two kiss like Mike Tyson punches."

"And he punches like he kisses," Pop added.

"You got it," Riskin nodded.

UNDER FRIENDLY FIRE

Holt abruptly got up from his chair, announced to the room: "All right, team, listen up. This here old fella was *my* high school coach." He put his arm around Pop. "He taught me everything I know about football, about baseball, about basketball. So when your old man asks you what you learned from *me* and you tell him not a damned thing, I want you to blame it on this old fella right here 'cause that's what he taught me: nothing."

The team broke into rousing applause. Pop Daniels joined in himself.

"That's the damndest testimonial I ever got," he remarked to Riskin.

The rest seemed easy. Riskin outlined his vision of *Pop Daniels' Dugout & Sports Bar* with Breezy's help. The satellite dish would get things going in the right direction, but there would also be Special Event nights with sports-trivia quizzes and celebrity roasts of former Dexter greats as well as a sports gameroom where the long-closed poolroom had been. Best of all, there would be a poured-concrete roadway leading up to the *paved* parking lot. For money, Riskin advanced, he had virtually every cent he made while sweating it out in the Gulf those long months except for what he spent on meals since his return and the Rustic's ecomony rates for long-term renters. Breezy would be receiving a lump sum from the life insurance in addition to her monthly military widow's compensation for as long as that would last, but Riskin promised that the lion's share of all that would go into escrow or whatever else she wanted to do with it. She did not like to be told what to do with her money but he was not hearing any of it. As far as the Sports Bar was concerned, only an amount matching his was acceptable to him in terms of her own investment in the proposition.

Holt sparked to the idea at once, even countering Pop's claim that he had been salting away a small fortune with fanatical frugality by claiming it was not a fortune at all but only what he had been able to save because there was nothing he really wanted beyond the new four-by-four he purchased every two years. The Sports Bar idea was the first of its sort to appeal to him since his abortive attempt to become a partner in a car dealership a few years back. In fact the idea appealed to him so much that he promised to call an old college buddy, originally a Phys-Ed major like himself, who was now practicing law in Atlanta. Buzz, he said, could do a quick search of state laws regarding satellite dishes, if there were any, and even present the case to the town council with Fallon himself in attendance. Buzz owed him one anyway, Holt asserted, for his having introduced him to his second wife.

UNDER FRIENDLY FIRE

As for Pop Daniels, he did not have much to add to the discussion except to say he was having a hard time believing what his ears were hearing.

Chapter 16

Morning

UNDER FRIENDLY FIRE

SIXTEEN

The alarm went off in Breezy's head. It was six-thirty. It was also Saturday morning and the first thought that occurred had something to do with him. Jimmy. It had a nice friendly sound to it, fit him real well. He fit her well. Jimmy Riskin. That was okay, too. Riskin. What was Jimmy riskin'? She played with the word in her sleepy, happy state. Jimmy was riskin' the same thing she was riskin'. The risk did not seem too great. He was easy to like and fun to be with if you let him get to know you.

Whitney Fallon had let him get to know her and she had come back. It has bothered her. But today she would not let things bother her. Last night, early this morning were golden. Just being at the football game watching Jimmy was fun. And going back to Pop's Bar again *without* Zed did not affect her as she thought it would because she was with *him*. Maybe something would even come of it, who knows, with

Jimmy's sports bar idea. Maybe it was a notion that would hold up for him, for all of them after the beer wore off.

It had not been the same way with Zed, not at first anyway. His appeal for her had been as much a tribute to the adulation that the kids heaped upon him for his football exploits as it had been a testimony of his animal magnetism. That was something that came later, grew on her. It was difficult for her to discern what percentage his popularity had to do with even that, and what part could be credited to her own personal familiarity with Zed. The lines were pretty blurred.

But she *had* loved him. There was no mistaking *that,* she admitted as she rolled lazily on her side. Would it have lasted? She could not answer that. True, it seemed to be getting better between them before he shipped out. She *had* prayed to have a child by Zed, a child that would have cemented the bond between them, she thought. But it was still too difficult to say. They had not a child. And if they had, forever was the longest--she stopped to count the letters--seven letter word she knew.

It was just easier with Jimmy. And certainly a lot clearer. Jimmy Riskin was nobody in Dexter. Far from being popular, he was an outsider, an absolute unknown when she had taken to him. Hell, she smiled, *that* happened on the first night she had seen him in

UNDER FRIENDLY FIRE

The Hopper, and ignored him outside her trailer, walking right past him. Peer pressure had nothing to do with the turnaround in her pursuit of him. No. *He* had pursued her. It was Jimmy who came to the diner the next morning to talk to her. Then *she* had left him high and lonesome at the Rustic during Patsy Cline, only to approach him again at The Hopper. Breezy laughed out loud in the morning stillness. The lines were getting blurrier and blurrier.

There was a knock on her front door. Suddenly she thought of that Vicki Carr song her Aunt Mimi used to love. "Dear God, it must be him," it went and she knew, she absolutely knew. Instinctively, she threw off Zed's old football jersey, put on a brown-and-yellow-check shirt, ran to the door in her bare feet, opened it.

It was Jimmy.

He did not say a thing, just stepped inside, pulled her to him and kissed her. She had not finished buttoning the shirt and she was glad. He was *unbuttoning* it, his mouth never leaving hers, his hands working anxiously, gently. She felt herself being lifted off the carpet, carried back into the bedroom, placed down on the soft white sheets. It was just too nice, too lazy-Saturday-morning nice; it made her want to help. She started unbuttoning *his* shirt. He let her; he was too busy applying gentle kisses to the curve of her neck, her bare shoulder. She was taking off his shirt, throwing it on the foot of the bed on top of hers.

With Jimmy it was just so easy. You did not have to do a thing, she let herself go completely. No man could be this gentle and still reach this far inside her. He made her feel--she tried to define it--the *luckiest*, that was it, she had ever felt.

Jimmy Riskin, where have you been all this time? When she remembered she sealed it all out, the Gulf, the war, even Zed. She threw herself back into the moment, the sensation of his skin against her skin, the gentle rhythm of their free swaying bodies, his upon hers, hers upon his. Breezy, you are Lucky now, she told herself, and, Jimmy, *you* have made the difference. Can you ever, ever forgive me for being so mean to you when I first met you? Will you let me make it up to you, not just today, but tomorrow and the day after? The questions were as silly, she knew, as she felt, their answers as simple as he was making them. Saturday morning is not the time for talk about forgiveness, he was telling her in his gentle, moving way, but a time for forgetting everything but what matters most.

In her life, in the shortest of times, she now admitted to herself, nothing had come to mean more than Jimmy Riskin. And the most amazing thing to her was that it did not scare her, did not intimidate her at all. With Zed, she had tried; with Jimmy, she would

UNDER FRIENDLY FIRE

try even harder, because she did not have to try at all, he had been that good to her.

"Jimmy," she spoke his name aloud. He heard her and was answering in his quiet breathing, his almost reverent touch. She heard *him*, felt his touch upon her and in her, in places no one had ever been.

Nothing could have been more natural than to find Jimmy there in those places, in this bed, on this morning.

"I know it's awful short notice," he was telling her after, as she cuddled in the crook of his bare arm, "but I thought I would drive up to Indiana and see my folks. I'd like you to come with me." He quickly added: "Not to meet them so much but because it's a long drive and I'd like to have you with me."

"Jimmy," she laughed like a little girl, "after this morning, you would have one heck of a time convincing me not to follow you to hell." It was not something a little girl would say, but it was something Breezy would say.

He kissed her hair, the bridge of her nose.

"If you knew my dad," he laughed back, "you'd know how appropriate that remark sounds."

"Come on, he can't be that bad; nobody is."

"He's *not* either, really, but me not being a soldier anymore might supply just the right effect."

"He does know already, doesn't he?"

MICHAEL CORNELL

"He knows I was considering doing it," Riskin said, "but considering's not the same as doing it."

"It really worries you, doesn't it?"

"No, it doesn't."

"Yes, it does."

"Yes, it does," he acknowledged with an uneasy smile. "So what about it: "Do you want to follow me into hell or not?"

"Can I take a shower first?"

"Is the water hotter than it is *there?*"

"You'll have to follow me in to find out," she kissed him on the mouth.

"When I'm good and ready," he kissed her back, drew her even closer.

"You're good and--"

"Don't say it," he whispered.

The shower could wait, would have to wait.

The water was just right. It was just funny to her to be sharing the tiny shower stall with anybody she had known for such a little while. Not really, she corrected herself. Jimmy was not just anybody and she had known him all her life it seemed, or maybe in a previous one, who could say. Not her. His hands, the rich lather felt too good.

Abruptly, the water pressure dropped.

"Old trailer," she apologized, "Auxiliary tank."

UNDER FRIENDLY FIRE

They finished their shower, toweled each other down.

"Does it come back up?" he asked.

"I don't know, does it?" she giggled, the bad little girl again.

"I mean the tank."

"I know what you mean." She tried to wipe the smile off her face, she did not know why. "The pressure will build up again."

He threw the towel aside, said: "I think it already has."

"What about your dad?"

"He wouldn't be interested." He pulled her close again.

"Who said a man is only as good as his last meal?"

"I give."

"Are you always this amorous before breakfast?" she had to know.

"Don't blame *me*," he kissed her nose again. "Blame the inspiration."

"Let me count the ways," she mused out loud. "The bed, the shower, now standing up."

"But we didn't do anything in the shower," he smirked.

"We didn't?"

"I mean..." his voice trailed off.

"I know what you mean," she laughed low, savoring his nakedness next to hers.

"Listen," he told her in the same low tone, "I want you to make the supreme sacrifice for me today."

"Just tell me what the supreme sacrifice is and order two," she returned, running her hands down his back, along his thighs.

"I know it's Saturday and all that, and it's a long ride, but the short little thing you wore the first time you stormed out of the Rustic..."

"And the high heels..."

"And the high heels, I'd like you to wear that on our way up to Indiana. What you wear once we get to my folks' house, I don't care."

She did not try to suppress her laughter. "Jimmy, by the time we leave here this morning--if we ever leave--you're liable to be so sick of me, you'll never want to see me again."

Now *he* laughed. "Maybe so, but is it all right if I keep coming around to sleep with you?"

Chapter 17

Illusions

UNDER FRIENDLY FIRE

SEVENTEEN

Riskin could not stop looking at her legs. The apricot mini, riding well up her naturally as she sat in the passenger seat, did not hide an inch of them. If he leaned over to tune in another station on the broken radio, he could catch a glimpse of the silken crotch of her panties. She did nothing to help that except wear them instead of those awful *men's* cotton underwear women were wearing nowadays to be like all the guys. Breezy McLachin was *not* one of the guys. Not in that dress, with those legs. It did not make for safe driving, he thought to himself, it made for *inspired* driving.

"What did you think of me when you first saw me," she uncannily or not so uncannily followed his train of thinking, "when you saw me taking off my clothes on that table in The Hopper?"

"Well, to be truthful--" he stopped short.

"Be truthful," she said.

"After I met some of your wonderful neighbors," he started up again with some reluctance, "I thought it was...was right in character."

"They painted that pretty a picture?" She was not surprised.

"It was something like the menu board at the diner," he decided to go the rest of the way, "pick a number and wait your turn."

Breezy looked out her window, finally spoke: "Since Zed died, that's what everybody wanted to think so that's what I let them think. The football hero was dead, so why not kill the Homecoming Queen with him. I hated to see such a logical plot destroyed so I kind of decided I would be the last person to destroy it. People around here need something to believe in besides high school football and the Fallons, so who was I to destroy their damn illusions."

Illusions? Is that what they were, he wanted to ask.

"They *were* illusions," she answered without his saying anything. "Would it have mattered terribly to you"

"Then, no. Now, a lot."

"I'm glad," she smiled, looking at him. "You're the first man I've let kiss me, much less touch me, since Zed."

He wanted to believe that.

UNDER FRIENDLY FIRE

"You can believe that if you want, because it's true." She *was* uncanny. "As they say, I was running but I wasn't hiding. Ask my wonderful neighbors, as you called them, or anybody who's a regular at The Hopper and that's just about everybody in Dexter who's got a libido left or think they do. Breezy McLachin was right there every night for everybody to see, the grieving war widow who didn't know the first thing about grieving or so it looked."

She was gazing out the window again, continuing: "Hell, she was up and around within a week and a half of her folks getting mangled in their station wagon by that semi. Sure, she was gallivanting around with her vampy Aunt Mimi who came to stay with her after they buried them, raising holy hell, still barely scraping by in school with low C's and high D's. What did that matter anyway? Everybody with half a wit knew she was just going to marry Zed McLachin the football star as soon as she graduated. It didn't take anybody with an IQ to know that. But what did you expect from the only kid of a drunken trucker who worked for that bastard brother of Whitney Fallon, Ricky Lee Powers, and whose mother--mine, not his--was just the prettiest little thing to leave South Tennessee without a brain to her name since they paved the Interstate."

Now he was not certain that she was talking to him. He did not think she was and he began looking for a place to stop.

MICHAEL CORNELL

"Who can blame her for giving them what they want? When you got nothing, you got nothing to lose, isn't that how the song goes? So Breezy scraped by with the first diploma in the whole damned history of her family and hitched her star to Mister Football and lived in a little tin trailer and washed his shorts and spread her legs anytime he felt like it. It's so bad it would make a good tv movie."

Some kind of wooded rest spot was coming up, thank God. He slowed the Jeep.

The sign read: *Colonel Reston Memorial Picnic Ground.* Not Grounds. It made sense to him as they approached. The area was too small to be a picnic *grounds.* He turned in anyway, pulled past the log fence, parked in one of the six slots, all available.

"Let's walk," he said.

The path led nowhere, not to a nature trail, not to a trickling brook. Colonel Reston would be smoking if he knew, Riskin thought.

"Are you about through?" he asked her.

She was taken aback, did not answer.

"When you're in that juke joint Hopper, you can drown in all the stinking beer you want," he let loose, "but when I asked you to be with me coming up here, I didn't ask you to be the damn homecoming queen who married the damn football hero and didn't amount to a damn thing. I asked you to be with me as you are, as I know you are, as you were in bed with me this morning or, hell, with me last night with Pops and Holt while be babbled on about some stupid or maybe not so stupid scheme I had about a sports bar and the reason maybe we all should pool together but *especially* you and me."

The way she listened so intently, so eloquently, almost steered him off his track. Almost.

"I've got this feeling, see," he resumed, "and I think you *do* see, because maybe, just maybe, you'll get the same feeling, too--" It was just too much to believe, to hope for that someone as beautiful as Breezy was beautiful could have that feeling, too, about *him,* Jimmy Riskin--"but whether you ever do or not, and maybe it'll be someone you haven't even met yet, for these two days that you're stuck with me, I only ask that you *be* with me or at least try like hell to fake it."

He wanted to touch her again, all over again, but suddenly he was afraid to muss her up. *Nobody* had that right, not even if she let them.

She kissed him.

She was giving him that right, letting him if he wanted to.

This moment in time in Colonel Reston's Picnic Ground with no nature trail and not even a trickling brook, Jimmy Riskin had *no* right to as much as think about laying a dirty hand upon her. This morning was this morning, he thought. This very small, inconsequential stop in time, he could only worship at the alter of her beauty. It was profane for him to even think otherwise.

"We've got a long way to go," he simply said now and started back, hoping she would not follow and he would have to look back at her face, her breasts, her legs in that slip of a dress she had worn for *him*.

"Jimmy." She reached out her hand.

He took it without turning, walked slowly ahead up the path.

The rest of the way, past the state line, into Indiana, into Indianapolis, was passed in simple statements, quiet conversation as though between two passengers on an Amtrak train who met each other at another time and had not forgotten but were merely saving and savoring the waiting moment when the train would stop and let all the other passengers off so that they could be alone to tell each other that they had not only not forgotten but had *never* forgotten.

Jimmy Riskin could never forget. He wanted the train to stop, to be rid of the responsibility of telling his father what he had to tell him and be on his way with *her,* lighting a vigil light before her sacred image and praying to sin again with her as before.

"Breezy," he managed to look across at her in the fading twilight, "thank you for being with me."

UNDER FRIENDLY FIRE

The woman who smiled back at him had never even heard of the godforsaken place called The Hopper, had never set foot in a trailer before, had never known anybody with a name the same as the last letter in the alphabet.

He could not wait to meet her.

Chapter 18

Indiana

UNDER FRIENDLY FIRE

EIGHTEEN

Jimmy looked more like his mother, Breezy thought as she smoothed out the safe, sedate blue dress she now wore. His mother had the same less-severe shape to her face, the same sandy-brown hair. Too, she was a hell of a lot calmer, more accepting than his old man.

"I'm not one to be telling you, Jimmy," his father was telling him in a voice that was louder than reason, "but you just can't be leaving one thing and not have another thing to go to."

At first, she thought he was hard of hearing; like Zed's father, he did look a lot older than his wife.

"I just wished we had talked, Jimmy," he seemed to conclude, looking at *her* on the cheap new sofa with Mrs. Riskin.

"We did talk, Dad," Jimmy said, "don't you remember?"

MICHAEL CORNELL

The old man had not concluded at all. "On the telephone is no way," he retorted, "not like eyeball to eyeball, man to man."

Breezy wished he would *stay* retired like he was supposed to be.

"And again I'm not one to be telling you, Jimmy," he was on to that line another time, "but who *is* this you're having us meet here?"

The man was not hard of hearing, she said to herself, he was hard of thinking. How many ways can someone be introduced. Jimmy was still trying to come up with another: "Breezy was the boy-I-told-you-about's wife," he informed him this time, "and I didn't bring Breezy here to meet you and Mom like that, she's just traveling with me, that's all.

"Breezy was married to the boy, dear," Mrs. Riskin now tried to explain to him.

"I *know* that," he raised his voice even higher. "If she was the boy's wife, I guess she was *married* to him. I just want to know what she's doing here."

"Breezy came close to saying something, but Jimmy was too quick: "Listen, Dad, if you're going to start telling me who I should be with or shouldn't be with," he rebuffed him, "then I have no business even coming here anymore."

"Jimmy, don't you ever say that," his mother cut in. "You know you're always welcome here in your home."

UNDER FRIENDLY FIRE

"But it's not my home anymore," he said and, for the first time, Breezy saw he was talking with his beautiful hands as well. "Mom, Dad, I love you, I love you both, but I've got to do some things, find out some things about myself, don't you understand?"

His father actually lowered his voice: "I know you do, Jimmy, but just don't let a mistake you made in the war--a mistake you weren't even responsible for--rule your thinking and ruin your life."

"Dad, I *was* responsible," Jimmy asserted straight out, "we were all responsible but nobody was more to blame than I was."

"Keep your voice down, son," his old man had the audacity to tell him. "In war, nobody's responsible for anybody else, it's just the nature of the damn thing."

"Then *you* tell that to Breezy, she's the one who doesn't deserve to hear that crap!"

They all looked at *her*. She felt like she was wearing the apricot mini-dress again, less.

Jimmy put his beautiful, expressive hands on his father's shoulders. "Dad, I didn't do what I did, leave the Army and the rest of it, *just* because of what happened in the war; I left it because I had to know some things about what I'm doing here and where I'm going to and there was no other way to find those things out." He added with a poignancy that stopped her, stopped them all: "Your little boy's been sleeping in the top bunk for too long, it's time he came down and started being *responsible* for what he does and *how* what he does affects other people."

He kissed his father on the mouth and, for once, his old man was not one to be telling him anything.

Chapter 19

Wild Card

UNDER FRIENDLY FIRE

NINETEEN

It was not one of your better neighborhoods in Indianapolis. It was not even one of your better *black* neighborhoods, Jimmy Riskin thought. It just did not matter to him. Card Mayes was the best friend he ever had in this city and the best damned basketball player he ever went up against.

He knocked on the door, looked at Breezy, now dressed in tight jeans and one of *his* sweatshirts. She did not seem too concerned about where they were and if whites had any business being around there at night or at anytime. He liked that.

Mayes came to the door himself, rubbed his eyes, said: "What the hell you doing here, white boy?" On the outside he was playing it dead serious.

"I'm looking for a black boy named Card Mayes," Riskin returned the straight tone. "They used to call him *Wild Card Mayes* when he thought he knew something about basketball."

MICHAEL CORNELL

"I'll see if he's around, smart boy." He let them into the old, modestly but neatly furnished house. There were too many little brothers and little sisters of his to be living under the same small roof, Riskin could see at once. He did not care; neither did Mayes. They abruptly grabbed each other, embraced in front of everyone. Breezy, the rest of Card's family just watched. Next, they listened to where each had been, what each had been doing, Riskin fighting the War in the Gulf, Mayes the war in the streets, a basketball scholarship gone sour on bad grades, job layoffs, the usual.

Then Card asked about Breezy. Riskin told him everything about her except how they met, why they met. Card's oldest sister spirited her away to show her around. There was no reason for either to stall the main agenda, not any longer.

"Been playing any?" Card wanted to know.

"Some, but against weak competition," Riskin made no bones about it.

"*White* competition you mean?" He was grinning that in-your-face grin opposing players could never forget.

"You talk as if I could find some action around here," Riskin smiled back.

"Anytime you want, white boy."

"The game's in your court, black boy," he accepted the challenge.

UNDER FRIENDLY FIRE

In minutes, they were all piling in Mayes' old Olds and Riskin's Jeep. In less than that, they were down the street in a vacant lot with a single street light beaming down from a crooked pole. Card opened his trunk, took out a brand new orange hoop with net attached. He boosted his smallest brother on his tall shoulders and the youngster screwed it into place at regulation height.

"You can always tell the black neighborhoods from the white neighborhoods," he laughed. "In the black 'hoods, the nets are always ripped away; in the white 'hoods, they're always still up 'cause the white boys can't reach 'em."

Riskin had heard it a few times, but it was still funny. Funnier than the first game of one-on-one. His warmups against the varsity players from Dexter High had not come close to preparing him. Mayes put some shake-and-bake moves on him that left him flat-footed like the Average White Basketball Player was supposed to be. To his credit, Wild Card never laughed; he just blew him away in a real laugher with Riskin putting only two down by the time Mayes had twelve and the game.

He was rustier than he guessed, which was okay, he thought, but *not* while Breezy was watching, not to mention Wild Card's cheering section which was growing by the point. It was no longer Riskin versus

Mayes and Family but Riskin against Mayes and the entire 'hood.

"You had enough?" Card offered as they slugged down two-liters of Pepsi from the same bottle.

"You ever think of joining the Army?" Riskin said out of the deep blue.

"This some kind of psychological ploy?" Mayes shot back.

"Uh-uh, it just occurred to me," he replied. "Sure did me a hell of a lot of good."

"Everywhere but out there," Card pointed to the lighted hoop.

"Yeah, well, they didn't have too many parquet courts in the desert," Riskin smirked, "but every place else it helped."

He actually seemed to be thinking about it. Then he said: "Guess I should tell my fans to disperse, though, is that it?"

"Why in hell would you do that," Riskin suddenly felt cocky, "Unless you're ducking a rematch."

"You're either crazy or doped, white boy."

In the return engagement, Riskin played like both. It was ten-all when he juked Mayes out of his Nikes and drove right past him for an easy lay. Then he stopped him on solid *D*, and put him away with a rainbow jumper that touched nothing but net.

Wild Card, the whole 'hood was impressed. Riskin was better than that: he was through for the

UNDER FRIENDLY FIRE

evening, having salvaged a hard-fought stand-off with the very best he had ever faced.

On the downside, Breezy was hardly watching the rematch, she was too immersed in conversation with Mayes' oldest sister.

Anyway, Wild Card *was* watching, Riskin took heart. There wasn't much else he could do but watch.

Chapter 20

Flight

UNDER FRIENDLY FIRE

TWENTY

Her father had taken her to a rent-a-carnival like this one, complete with Ferris wheel, carousel and kiddie rides when she was a little girl. Otherwise, it was like a date from an old black-and-white Lana Turner movie. They had spotted the doings on the way back to Dexter in a place nothing had been only the day before. Riskin had insisted that they should stop. He had also bought the cotton candy and won her the Taiwan kewpie doll at pitch-and-toss. The only essential difference between this and the Lana Turner starrer was that Jimmy Riskin was standing in for John Garfield. In the pleasant Sunday evening glow, it was a difference Breezy McLachin could live with.

"How'd you get so cute?" she asked Garfield's stand-in as they strolled toward the dodge-'em cars.

"Practice," he replied succinctly.

The postman would not have rung *once* for lines like that but who was counting.

"Shall we?" Jimmy suggested as he witnessed a massive twelve-car pileup that claimed no fatalities but lots of laughs.

"*You* go," she said, somehow remembering her parents and the station wagon.

"And leave you with *my* cotton candy," he kidded. "Well, then *you* pick it."

She nodded her head in the direction of the Ferris wheel.

"You think you're dressed for it," he indicated the short, flouncy red-and-white thing she had on. She had brought enough things along for a week's trip but each seemed to supply the desired effect. "All right, these little boys around here have got to start learning sometime," he laughed.

It was when they had reached the zenith of the wheel's turn that she thought she saw a shooting star. It may have been just a reflection from the lights below but it made her recall her father telling her that seeing a shooting star was good luck. Jimmy Riskin was all the good luck she needed. Besides, he had promised to catch the next falling meteor anyway.

"*If* it's a change-up or a curve with not too much smoke on it," he grinned, then added one last disclaimer: "And *if* you promise to watch my next one-on-one with Wild Card."

UNDER FRIENDLY FIRE

"I *was* watching," she asserted.

"You were talking."

"I was watching while I was talking."

"Then tell me how I won it?" he wanted to know.

"Well..." she was trying to remember, "you went right past him and shot the ball in."

"That was the *second-last* point," he needled her with a little sharper point than she would have guessed. Sports, as with Zed, was pretty important to him. It was something else she could live with as the other parallels fell away.

The wheel was slowing down. It made her sad.

"I want to go again!" she blurted out and, at once, she knew she had had a lot of nerve questioning the little boy in him with his pickup basketball games. There were two lost kids riding the wheel.

"You're calling the shots," he acceded to her wish.

When they reached the heights again on the second ride, she kissed him. The wheel seemed to linger up there on its controlled flight. As she reopened her eyes, she thought she saw another shooting star, for sure this time.

"Did you see it!" the little girl in her asked him with child-like desperation. "Did you see it, too?"

"If you say I did," Jimmy smiled his quiet smile, "then I guess I did."

It was all she needed to hear.

Chapter 21

Home

UNDER FRIENDLY FIRE

TWENTY-ONE

It was the strangest thing, Jimmy Riskin said to himself. The sign reading *Dexter 2 Miles* looked good to him. Better than *Indianapolis 6 Miles* had looked. And a hell of a lot better than the *Welcome to Dexter* one with the *Friendliest City* crap and *Zed McLachin* epitaph had looked the first time he had driven in. But that was so long ago or such a short time ago he could not remember.

It was twenty to two Sunday night, Monday morning when he drove up behind Breezy's pickup and walked her to her door.

"I had a wonderful time this weekend, Jimmy," she said. "Thank you for asking me along."

He smiled. It sounded as though they had held hands at a church picnic. Hell, he thought, they had kissed at a carnival, on the top of the Ferris wheel.

MICHAEL CORNELL

He looked at her again. She was the girl from the *Seventeen* cover once more. He took hold of her, kissed her gently on her forehead, her nose, her mouth.

"Want to come in?" she asked.

It was a silly question. He almost said *Do horses like hay?* or something equally silly. He liked her silliness.

"You've got to get up in a few hours," he reminded her with a solicitude both could do without.

"Yeah, but I'll sleep better."

He followed her inside, kissed her again, longer, running his eager hands over the material of her red-and-white dress. The color was just a memory by the time he reached under.

They dropped to their knees on the living room carpet with only a tiny night-light illuminating each other, to read each other by. She reached beneath his shirt; he pulled the hem of her dress over her slender hips.

In moments, they were on the carousel again, at the very top, alone against the night sky, with only their quiet, pious breathing to disturb their perfect universe.

"I love *you*," one of them said, he could not be certain which.

They lay on the carpet, felt the soft grass of the gently rolling hills, the protection of the looming oak, the privacy of the indigo canopy above them. It was a

UNDER FRIENDLY FIRE

spot neither of them had ever been on a night neither had ever known, a night neither could ever let go.

"I love *you*," the other voice returned.

Neither had said it first.

Neither had said it last.

It was as it should be, he thought, and it would not have to be said again.

Chapter 22

Plans

UNDER FRIENDLY FIRE

TWENTY-TWO

A Limited Partnership Agreement was signed by all principals and notarized by the Dexter Fidelity Bank with Pop Daniels retaining controlling interest, Tim Holt buying in as a Class A voting partner, and Jimmy Riskin and Breezy McLachin owning smaller, equivalent shares for their lesser investments. The name was officially registered as *Pop Daniels' Dugout & Sports Bar* and work begun at once on the new paved road and parking lot. Paul ("Buzz") Blankenship was contacted by Holt at his Atlanta law office and commenced to dig into the fine-print legalities of satellite and cable television transmission. He promised to call back with his findings within a week's time and, if necessary, present them to the Dexter Town Council at their next month's meeting.

Riskin, meanwhile, moved out of the Rustic Motor Inn and into a three-room, furnished walk-up above Grant's Hardware which was owned and run by

MICHAEL CORNELL

Flaherty's sister and her husband. Everything and everybody was inter-related in some way in Dexter, Riskin was fast finding out. It made for a filial folksiness if you were born and raised there but took an exacting toll on privacy for strangers and non-strangers alike. Riskin still categorized himself as one of the former but the puzzling sensation of belonging to someplace for the first time made each day a more familiar experience to him. Owning a piece of Pop's Dugout, albeit a tiny one, augmented that feeling.

The apartment, it occurred to him, was really the first place of his own. The rooms and the well-worn but sturdy furniture may have been the property of somebody else, but the living space was his and his alone while he was there. For twenty-three years, he had lived under either his father's or the United States Army's roofs. Now, he would be heading off to work at Flaherty's service station from his own homebase and returning there each late-afternoon. Even that had a comfortable strangeness to it.

Riskin was carrying in some newly purchased pots and cooking utensils when he received his first visitor. She was waiting for him at the top of the stairs.

"Hello, Mrs. Fallon," he greeted her cordially as his surprise would allow.

UNDER FRIENDLY FIRE

"My, such formality in the face of familiarity," she laughed her refined laugh, "especially in light of such a friendly *open-door* policy."

"I left the downstairs door open because I was hauling things up that I bought at the hardware," he explained, placing his packages down to unlock the apartment door.

Whitney Fallon stood in his way, said: "Not until I get a kiss."

He did not have to kiss her to gain admittance to what belonged to him. He kissed her because, after staring at blackened, oily car engines all day, he could not help himself, she looked so well-scrubbed, genteel, inviting. He hated himself after, more than Breezy Mclachin could have hated him at that moment.

"Mind if I come in?" she asked in her warmest, aristocratic tone. There was a contradiction in there somewhere, he thought, maybe a few hundred.

"Sure." He opened the door, let her in.

"Aren't you even going to offer me a drink in your new place?" she inquired as he immediately started to put the cooking gear away.

"There's a beer in the icebox," he called from the kitchen, "But it's probably not your brand."

There was no reason to call out; Whitney was standing four feet away from him, touching, not leaning against, the refrigerator.

"I talked to Ricky Lee," she informed him. "You remember, my stepbrother?"

"How could I forget Ricky Lee *or* his business associates," was Riskin's comeback.

"I saw you at the football game, you know," Whitney changed categories, "you and Breezy McLachin."

He took out a can of beer, snapped open the top.

"Aren't you going to give me one of those?" she asked.

"I don't have any glasses yet."

"Well then, I'll just have a sip of yours."

Riskin reopened the refrigerator, put the beer back.

"Listen, Whitney, I don't think this is such a good idea anymore," he said, closing the door, looking straight at her.

"Oh, but you thought Fallon's Point *was* a good idea at the time," she responded, the refinement, the control still there.

"Not the *last* time I didn't." It was a weak return, but he did not care.

"What would you say if I told you that I was thinking of leaving my husband, taking Brandon away with me and leaving for good?" The control seemed to slip with the revelation.

UNDER FRIENDLY FIRE

"I'd say it was a decision you'd have to make yourself, without any outside help or coaching," he answered.

"Coaching," she sounded the word out. "That's funny: sports analogies for all occasions."

The remark made him feel uneasy; he should have felt uneasier.

"I'm sorry I bothered you," she said and left.

Riskin listened to the front door close, then wondered why he had not seen the Jaguar or her minivan downstairs at the curb. Maybe she parked it around the corner, or two blocks away, so Ricky Lee would not get suspicious. Or so Rance Fallon would not put the proverbial two and two together and come up with something that made as much sense as Whitney Fallon and Jimmy Riskin.

That evening during an informal planning meeting at The Dugout, Riskin saw Rance Fallon for the first time. Everyone was present except Breezy who had her aunt from Memphis staying over for the night. Daniels, Holt and Riskin were reviewing the costs of basic requirements for the new gameroom when Fallon entered alone. Pop excused himself to talk to the man, Dexter's Mayor, while Holt and Riskin continued discussion on the gameroom. Throughout, Riskin continued to watch Fallon, study him.

MICHAEL CORNELL

Like Whitney, he had a polished look about him. Unlike Whitney, the veneer seemed put on, made up. In another time, Fallon could have been a leading man in B-movies or a second banana in A ones, the rival of the lead. He was handsome to be sure, but it was the almost too-perfect handsomeness that spoke of silver soup plates or ivory cigarette holders. Riskin could not imagine the man ever shooting basketballs in a sweaty T-shirt or getting in a real fistfight over his prom date's honor. But those were appearances; maybe the facade was thicker than it looked. For some reason, it made Riskin think of what his father always used to say about the Army: they'll give you the benefit of the doubt as long as they doubt you'll benefit. Rance Fallon meant nothing to him, even less than before, and now he was leaving anyway.

When Daniels returned to the table, Holt asked him what Fallon wanted.

Characteristically, Pop said damned if he knew or words to that effect.

Chapter 23

Mim

UNDER FRIENDLY FIRE

TWENTY-THREE

No woman Mimi Miller's age had any business looking as good as she did without a heartfelt debt to a skilled plastic surgeon. Mimi never knew one; her share of oil men and car dealers, even the owner of a major league ballteam, but no plastic surgeons. Perhaps, Breezy thought, her aunt's youthful appearance was nothing more than a lingering testament to the woman's strict lifelong regimen of cigarettes and Miller Beer. Whatever it was, Breezy hoped to hell she had it when she caught up to Aunt Mimi chronologically. It was the *only way* she could ever catch up.

"Not another soldier," Mimi was berating her goodnaturedly, the ubiquitous cigarette and can of Miller's in the same hand. "You'll never achieve financial prosperity that way, Breez."

"And you have with your Memphis wholesale man, Mim?" Both always cut off the endings to each other's names. "Besides, he's not a soldier *anymore*."

"Once one, always one." Mim liked the sound of her own retort, Breezy could tell by the extra long sip of beer she took. "It's a way of thinking they get that they can never really shake," she said after swallowing.

"Jimmy doesn't think that way at all," Breezy assured her.

"You don't even know which way I was talking about," her aunt insisted. "You see, they can never quite picture themselves as being free--so they really aren't."

"What's free, Mim? If you mean he knows he's got to work, to make money to live and eat, then nobody's free."

"That's not the kind of freedom I'm talking about, Breez," the woman objected again. "I'm talking about his feelings for you."

"I don't want him to think he's free from me," she responded, then added: "not entirely."

"Well, maybe right now when everything is new, he won't want to be free from you, Breez." Now Mim took an extra-long drag of her diminishing cigarette. "But someday he might just want to bust out completely, when it dawns on him that he's *not* wearing that olive-drab monkey suit no more. And sometimes someday comes a lot sooner than it ever oughtta. *I* know."

For the first time Breezy detected a hint of sadness in her aunt's voice. It did not stop her from going on: "Do you think I left Dexter with Irvin the day after you married Zed McLachin because I thought he was some damn knight on a shining horse?" she resumed in the same tone. "Hell, no. Give me credit for more smarts than that, Breez. And give me credit, too, for not believing that Irvin was gonna be able to pull off even fifteen percent of the financial transactions he was always bragging about, from Ollie North masks to some goofy Barbie-Doll lookalikes made in Taiwan. Well, any idiot could've told you those cheap things weren't gonna make anybody anything but trouble, in copyright infringements alone."

"So Irvin fell off the horse, eh, Mim?" Breezy knew she should not have been making light of the conversation but she could not resist.

"Well, let's just say he stumbled out of the gate a few times," the woman chuckled, seeming to lighten up herself. "So Irvin might not win or place too many times but on my card he's always gonna show."

"And Jimmy isn't?"

"Maybe he is and maybe he isn't," Aunt Mim concluded and Breezy was certain the point was lost somewhere between the gulps of beer and the puffs of smoke.

"So what do you want to do tonight, Mim?" Breezy left the point behind. "You're my guest tonight and you're calling the shots."

"The hell with the shots, the beer's fine," the woman rose on her shapely, shaky legs. "Let's you 'n' me go set the woods on fire like that Hank Williams song goes."

Aunt Mim made her way unsteadily into the bedroom and Breezy could hear her going through the wardrobe.

"I'm traveling light, so I gotta wear something of yours, Breez," she called out.

"You know all of my things still fit you, Mim," Breezy called back.

"Whooee!" her aunt abruptly whistled and returned to the living room holding up the blue velvet evening dress. "This must have set some horny sonofabitch back some pretty cash."

"Jimmy bought that for me," Breezy said quietly, suddenly wishing she could be with him, just the two of them, not saying anything, just being in the same place. She could not, they could not. Aunt Mim was in Dexter just for the night and the night belonged to her.

If the Judds had raided the Pointer Sisters' trailer, it would have still fallen short of approximating the

UNDER FRIENDLY FIRE

look of Breezy and her Aunt Mim in tandem one half hour later. Breezy, in a form-hugging mini out of the Sixties, was flashy; the older woman, in a mix-and-match out of a street walker's nightmare, was flashier. The possibilities were boundless, the results merely hypothetical.

Mim passed out from beer consumption before they hit the door, leaving Breezy to wonder if her forty-eight year-old aunt had finally passed puberty, after all, right there on her trailer floor.

Chapter 24

Reachable Dreams

UNDER FRIENDLY FIRE

TWENTY-FOUR

"If this isn't the happiest day of my life, I'll be damned if I can remember one that beats it," Pop Daniels was telling Jimmy Riskin as he feasted his good eye on the overflow crowd. The old coach had reason to be elated. Everything had come together as fast as he could have imagined, faster. The poured concrete roadway and parking lot, the new neon sign, the gameroom addition, the huge satellite dish. Especially the satellite dish. Buzz Blankenship's legal papers in Tim Holt's hands had sufficed to stonewall Mayor Fallon and his town council at this month's open meeting. They had even started some Dexterites to predicting that a cable franchise could not be far behind, even if Fallon himself would be controlling the action.

Riskin had taken to watching Breezy McLachin moving assuredly through the customers in her tight-fitting, apricot jumpsuit. In his mind he was taking some pleasure and maybe a little credit, when Whitney Fallon walked up, escorted by none other than Rance Fallon. It was the real-life equivalent of the man from the song who danced with his wife in Chicago. Fallon was doing the congratulating: "I don't know just how much you had to do with this, Riskin, but you're to be commended," he stated smoothly, extending a hand. Riskin wondered how he even knew his name, shook the hand just the same. There was no reason not to, not yet anyway. "I'd introduce you to my wife, but she tells me the two of you already met."

Riskin looked at her, trying to hide the surprise.

"I told you, Rance dear," Whitney began, all poise and grace, "Jimmy Riskin was the boy who fixed my problem for me, with the Jaguar."

It was an intriguing way to put it, Riskin thought, and he had been called worse things.

"You know about these special makes, do you?" was Fallon's follow-up question.

"When you've been around cars like I have--" he started to say before the Mayor cut him off.

"Yes, but how long have you been around Dexter?" Fallon wanted to know instead. "And how long do you intend to stay?"

Riskin did not even bother with the first one. "I was thinking of settling here," he replied.

Fallon seemed to lower the facade, drop the pose. "That so," he said. "It's so seldom that an outsider

UNDER FRIENDLY FIRE

takes to Dexter like that--and vice-versa, I might add." He was looking at his wife as he finished.

His Honor might have said good night and good luck as well, they both might have, but something else had caught Riskin's eye: a little green card with numbers, baseball scores on it. A customer with a Cub's cap on his head was scrutinizing one at the near end of the bar. So was a middle-aged couple at a nearby table. And a young guy in a softball uniform.

Riskin made his way over to the softball player, asked: "Where'd you get the betting card?"

"A guy gave it to me in the parking lot. He's passing 'em out to everybody."

Riskin called Tim Holt over, showed him the card. "You or Pop have anything to do with this?" he inquired, the urgency dripping.

"You think we like cutting our own throats?" Holt asked back.

"You collect them, every one of them, while I take care of the wiseguy who's passing these sonofabitching things out in our parking lot." Riskin sounded like he was back in uniform, giving the orders this time. Holt was not balking.

Riskin lit out of The Dugout just as the Fallon's red Jaguar was pulling away, spotted the short, brazen bastard handing out the green cards in the middle of the second parking aisle. In seconds, he had shorty by his choking throat.

"Who put you up to this?" he demanded.

The guy sputtered something to the effect that they were *his* cards, nobody put him up to it. He was taking his cards and the rest with the ink still drying on them that sat in the front seat of his beat-up Ford.

Riskin had collected the whole set just as local law turned into the newly paved parking lot of *Pop Daniels' Dugout & Sports Bar.*

As he watched her now, he was thinking of her coming over that first time at the diner and shutting him out, taking his order, nothing more. Now Breezy McLachin was staring out the window at the Van Gogh night. *His* window. His old roommate and bargain-basement art mentor Levine would have been amazed. *Reachable Dreams,* Levine called them. Sometimes they were impossible ones, Riskin thought, dreams you had no business ever reaching out for, you were just too dumb to know any better. This night he did not feel dumb; he felt as good as he ever felt. Like Pop, maybe better.

"So you think the betting cards were a plant?" Breezy was saying but in an abstract way, as though it were somebody else's problem.

It was. Certainly not Riskin's, not on this night. He came over, wrapped his arms around her small waist from behind.

UNDER FRIENDLY FIRE

"They never stood in the dark with you love..." he murmured, half-humming, half-mumbling.

"*Hold Me*, isn't it?" she somehow recognized the melody. "My Aunt Mim always liked that song."

"She liked that song and I like you."

"Do you really?" It was a silly, sensible response.

"What is this--*Double Jeopardy?*" he kidded, his hands now running south, now running north.

"Do you know what my Aunt Mim says?"

"What's the category?"

"She said you like me now, but that someday soon you might just want to bust out and break away."

"It just goes to show: Aunt Mim knows her music, but she doesn't know a thing about Jimmy Riskin."

He turned her around, kissed her gently above her blue eyes.

"You," he whispered, have changed everything for me. He wanted to say it now but something about what Levine had said about the dream being no good if it wasn't attainable stopped him. He did not know why, because he was holding it right now, tangible proof it *was* reachable. Levine was always claiming that you needed *tangible proof.* Riskin had it, he was certain of it.

"You have changed everything about my life," he said it out loud.

MICHAEL CORNELL

Breezy kissed *him*. There, Levine, take that: *Exhibit A*. What more tangible proof do you need?

The first thing in the morning he would try and reach his know-it-all Army buddy from the East, Riskin resolved, hoping morning would never come.

Chapter 25

Omen

UNDER FRIENDLY FIRE

TWENTY-FIVE

It felt good not to have to report to work until noon.

In the Saturday morning light, Ginny Walker's shack looked more dilapidated than ever. Yet, as the gold cast of the sun painted it, somehow it looked more hopeful, less desolate. Maybe she was projecting her own feelings, she thought, but what was so wrong about that? Things *were* changing and Ginny deserved much of the credit.

"I'm glad I listened to you," Breezy was saying.

"Wasn't nothing I done," the old woman returned, leaving the front door wide open to let the morning play inside. "You just started trustin' your own good luck and you acted on it, that's all. Though I was right about your Jimmy not bein' a mind-reader, wasn't I?"

"Maybe he is, maybe he isn't," Breezy smiled, "so I haven't left anything to chance. I took your advice and told him exactly how I feel. So far it's working fine."

"And it'll keep workin', too," Ginny assured her, then seemed to become somewhat preoccupied, as though she had misplaced something, something small but significant enough to disturb the pleasantness of the girl's visit. She began wringing her bony hands nervously.

"What is it, Ginny?" Breezy inquired with evident concern.

"Nothin' is wrong," the old woman lied, her eyes now directed in darting glances to the bare-board floor. "I just lost somethin', that's all."

"What did you lose?" Breezy insisted on knowing. When Ginny would not answer, she asked again, but with an urgency that seemed to sense something more than what was not being said. "Tell me what you lost."

"It was nothin'," Ginny lied again before finally disclosing: "It was just one of my Scrabble letters, that's all." She pointed to the pile of wooden anagrams on the card table.

"Which letter was it?" Breezy demanded.

"I---I don't know which letter it was," the old woman managed feebly.

Breezy rushed over to the table, sat down in one of the rickety chairs, frantically began sorting the tiles alphabetically.

UNDER FRIENDLY FIRE

"Sure glad your nerves don't need relaxin' now," Ginny tried awkwardly to make small talk and evade further questioning, "because these old grizzled hands of mine ain't much good for nothin' this mornin'---"
Breezy looked up from the sorted letters.
"Well, did you find which one was missin'?" old Ginny queried unconvincingly. "I probably just swept it under the bed or somethin' when I was cleanin' up last night."
Breezy just kept staring at her as she stood framed in the bright doorway.
"It's the 'Z', ain't it?" Ginny Walker now intoned gravely.
"The 'zed'," Breezy nodded, her eyes distant.
"But Zed's dead," the old woman stated.
It sounded more like a question.

Chapter 26

Levine

UNDER FRIENDLY FIRE

TWENTY-SIX

Levine could not be standing there. Riskin had not called him, but he was standing there in the entrance to the service bay in his Army dress greens with that same know-it-all Eastern smirk on his face.

"I knew I would find you here, Riskin," he said, narrowing his eyes, shaking his cocky head.

"Yeah, and how in the hell did you know that, Levine?" he countered. It was always Levine and Riskin. Riskin and Levine. They had no first names.

"How'd I know?" he repeated the question, picked up an empty can of oil additive. "S-T-P, that's how I knew," he deadpanned, tapping the can. "But I also talked to your dad long distance. He told me you were in and out of there."

"I was just thinking about you last night, Levine," Riskin finally marvelled.

"What happened: Somebody steal your Remington bronze? Well, Riskin, I wasn't thinking about *you* last night."

Maybe it was not coincidence at all, he thought. They had always been kindred spirits.

"Mrs. McLachin must really be something," Levine cracked out of leftfield. It was a position he played well.

"*Mrs.* McLachin?" For a moment Riskin really could not think of who that was. Then it dawned on him: "Oh, you mean Breezy?"

"Well, when I didn't hear a peep from you, I figured the old hormones must be at play," Levine joked. "Don't you remember telling me you were going to visit the merry widow. I already had the poor guy's name; the boys behind the desks fed me the rest."

"How long do you have?"

"I've got to be back to the base by roll call tomorrow morning, but I've been driving ten hours straight through so I have at least three or four hours to substantiate the whereabouts of my old Army pal."

"Pal? Hey, I wouldn't go that far, Levine," Riskin shot him a confirming grin as he wiped his hands on the last clean rag, notified Flaherty, and headed off to the last American diner with his old Army pal.

As Riskin guessed, Breezy took to Levine in the same way he did. You *had* to like somebody who could be cynical and funny at the same time.

UNDER FRIENDLY FIRE

"When I met this guy," Levine was telling Breezy, "the only Hopper he knew was Dennis and the only Remington he knew was an electric shaver."

"Sounds like we went to different schools together," Breezy laughed in a self-deprecating way that disarmed them both.

Levine threw an arm around Riskin, said in a tone that almost sounded serious: "Between now and the time we last saw each other, Riskin, where in hell did you acquire that kind of requisite charm to land a looker like this?" he added in a Marxian undertone, Groucho not Karl: "And as soon as I find out what the word 'requisite' means, I'll get back to you."

"Breezy, I don't believe it," Riskin returned serve, "I finally stumbled on something Levine is *not* taking credit for."

"*Stumble* is the operative term there, Riskin," Levine volleyed adeptly as Ted Bolan called over from the counter.

"Jimmy, it's Pop." Not one of them had even heard the phone as Levine was holding court. "Sounds like trouble at The Dugout."

Riskin rushed over, took the receiver. Levine was right behind him. Pop was running his words together excitedly, but Riskin got the message, said into the phone: "Call the school and tell Holt to bring along some of his players--tackles and linebackers, no backs or split ends. I'm on my way." He tossed the receiver to Bolan.

"Why didn't you tell me, Riskin," Levine volunteered, "I could've brought the 82nd Airborne with me."

Riskin and Levine were out of the diner before Breezy and Bolan could trade concerned glances. Levine pointed to the spanking new, black four-by-four parked across the street. It was twenty-two, twenty-three G's easily.

"How in hell did you swing this?" Riskin queried him as they hurried over.

"With my reenlistment bonus," Levine informed him, jumping behind the wheel.

"*You* reenlisted?" Riskin was floored as they roared off.

"You got it, pal," Levine smiled.

"What about your...your..." Riskin could not finish.

"My freedom, my independence?" Levine finished for him above the steadily mounting crescendo of the engine. "I'll have that in spades when I finish my book in three years. *Reachable Dreams*, remember?"

"How could I forget," Riskin answered and burst out laughing in absolute disbelief. He could not stop *until* they reached The Dugout.

The picture in the parking lot was not funny at all. Harleys lined up wheel to turned wheel.. Holt

UNDER FRIENDLY FIRE

arrived at the same time with two vanloads of strapping student-athletes who looked more like athlete-students, but he was not laughing either.

"See, if you can pick out the Dexter patrol car in the mess of chrome," he remarked to Riskin as the contingent headed toward the front door.

Inside, it could have been worse and was probably going to be. A couple of tables were turned over on top of some three-legged chairs, black spray paint streaked the walls and bar, and the green felt surface of the new pool table looked like yesterday's editorial, ripped to shreds. Other than that, the black leather jackets were behaving like little Angels.

As many as there were, when the other vanloads started arriving, there were more from the home-side. The fracas that ensued could best be described as *spirited,* better suited for *America's Craziest Videos* than for a Tyson undercard on HBO. The best punch of the melee was probably thrown by Levine, of all people, but the Angel who was on the receiving end was not coherent enough to vote. To his cohort's credit, it never came to tire irons and chains and, when it was over and the visitors were on their way, the whole affair had Riskin thinking that maybe the black leather jackets were just overgrown boys who wanted to have a little fun. When Holt conjectured that they might have been playing for pay, though, it stopped him so cold he blotted it out of his mind. He did not want to be thinking about Rance Fallon while he had the chance to be renewing acquaintance with his old friend Levine.

It was only after The Dugout was restored to some facsimile of order, that Riskin and Levine were able to pick up where they left off.

"I don't get it," Riskin was shaking his head. "*You* staying in the Army."

Levine was not apologizing. "The way I see it, I got one brother who is a lawyer, one sister who is an art director at a big ad agency; so what's wrong with one sibling being in the military? Where else could I get paid for the kind of adventure-of-a-lifetime that you and I went through in the Gulf. I tell you, Riskin, it was the stuff of books."

"Write your first one first, Levine," he suggested good-naturedly.

"I will, while I'm serving my second and last hitch, you watch," he insisted. "But what about *you?* You talk about *me* going straight-arrow. Here, you've settled your butt down in this little slice of Americana and--don't punch me in the nose, Riskin, now you sound like you're talking about something past going steady with this Breezy. I'm not saying I blame you, mind you..." His voice trailed off as he took the point as far as he could go.

Riskin was not making excuses either. "I'm not going to tell you Breezy is different from other women

UNDER FRIENDLY FIRE

I've known," he said, putting his beer down, "but she is. The first time I saw her she was stripping on top of a table."

"It's a long way from the Gulf, I guess," Levine observed wryly, "but you could've at least sent me a postcard."

"The funny part of it is," Riskin resumed, "*that* couldn't be further from Breezy than if you walked in here wearing a wedding gown."

"The only thing different about me is that for the first time I feel like I belong to something--"

"Or someone," Levine interjected cannily.

"That, too," Riskin smiled. "Maybe you ought to try it sometime, Levine."

"Maybe I will, Riskin," Levine held his empty Bud to the light, "but do you mind if I have another beer first?"

It only got better when Breezy arrived after work. The only shame of it was that the earlier one-round preliminary with the black leather jackets lasted only long enough to constitute one chapter of Levine's book. But knowing Levine, Riskin said to himself, he would *heighten* the hell out of it.

Chapter 27

Rain

UNDER FRIENDLY FIRE

TWENTY-SEVEN

By the time Breezy reached her trailer after they had seen Levine off, the rain was descending in torrential proportions. She pulled the sweater over her head and made a run from her truck to the trailer door, key in hand. Slipping it into the lock, she noticed a wadded piece of paper stuck between the bristles of the mat. She picked it up, pushed the door in.

Unravelling the paper, she read in barely legible pencil print:

>   Breezy
> Must see you
>   Ginny

Something cold shot up her back. The gusting wind could have dislodged the note from between the door and metal sill; it would not have crumpled it up.

Somebody did that. Something else: What in hell could have compelled old Ginny Walker to make her way on foot over the hills and through the high grass from her distant shack on a night like this one?

Breezy went to the bedroom, took a wrinkled raincoat from the wardrobe, slipped it on, pulling it over her head like a hood. She stuffed Ginny's note into the side pocket, left the dry security of the trailer.

As she now made her own way through the tall grass being combed wildly by the wind and rain, she fully expected to find the old woman lying collapsed on the ground before her. At her age, in her frail state, the journey must have represented the most strenuous of treks for Ginny; it was arduous enough for Breezy.

Breezy had always gone to see Ginny. Only once was it the other way around. There *was* a time not so long ago, she recalled. It was the night before she received the telegram.

Ginny Walker had had a premonition of some sort. It was sketchy, *muddled*, she had called it. She had taken out the little burlap pouch, had been drinking her papaya concoction, she had admitted, and was *jumbling* the wooden Scrabble letters.

M-C-L had come up on the first three letters. The first three letters of Zed's last name, McLachin, their name. The old women had panicked, rushed out of the shack, hurried over the hills as fast as her spindly legs could carry her. When she reached Breezy's trailer, she still carried the three wooden tiles in her bony hand.

"Are you *sure*, Ginny?" Breezy had wanted desperately to know.

"It's just three letters, girl," Ginny had shaken her ivory-haired head, "them's all that would come out. Maybe I shouldn't have come, maybe I should of. I thought you oughtta know what I know."

Then she had forced a laugh, said: "But I *don't* know. I can't know until..." She did not finish, Breezy remembered well.

The following morning a Marine courier delivered the telegram to her. He had announced something to the effect that he regretted to inform her--she could not remember him finishing either. He had been gone a full ten minutes before she even opened the pale-yellow envelope, actually read the telegram.

It had not been necessary. Ginny Walker had prepared her, informed her long hours before.

It was true that Ginny had said she could not be sure, that she could not know, but Breezy had known at once, right then looking at the letters.

She continued to push on through the driving rain, the impeding grass like Zed churning his way through tacklers toward the goal line, she thought. But once over the crest of the second hill, the highest slope, it was not Zed's end zone that beckoned but Ginny's ramshackle single-room house, barely illuminated through the frenzied mist by a single candlelight.

At least Ginny had made it back, she thanked God.

Breezy probably thought she heard the Coke-bottle chimes rattling in the small open windows well before she did, because she *wanted* to hear them. But why were the windows still open, why had Ginny not covered them with those old fruit-crate panels, she wondered in her confusion when she really could hear the old green bottles.

Emerging from the wind-tangled weeds, Breezy broke breathlessly for the front door, shoved it open violently.

Ginny was there, drenched upon her old Army cot, drenched in blood, her throat slit from one tiny ear to the other.

In a state born of unreasoning shock, Breezy McLachin unlocked the vise-like grip of Ginny Walker's small balled fist. In its wrinkly palm were three wooden letters.

She dropped to her knees, arranged them on the floor: Z-E-D.

The missing letter had turned up.

Chapter 28

Refuge

UNDER FRIENDLY FIRE

TWENTY-EIGHT

Reese McLemore was a jackdaw wimp. Why would any Marine try to duck real live combat on account of a lousy sprained wrist? Unless he had a candy-ass yellow stripe painted up his spine, why in the hell would he? Flat out, Reese McLemore was the root of all his trouble.

Zed McLachin was convinced of it.

He wished to hell he had never met the sonofabitch in that tent-top desert sick ward run by a bunch of jackasses better suited to be working at a bump shop than as mail-order medics. First they were dumb enough to stick *him* in there-- Zed McLachin, the high school All American who never missed a single minute of game time with an injury-- and try to confine him from seeing the start of ground action because of a little ankle sprain he got jumping out of an all-terrain vehicle. Then they were too dumb to distinguish between McLemore and himself when the two switched nametags and bunks so *that* lily-livered bastard would be able to duck combat while *he* jumped into it with both feet like any self-respecting Marine would. Of course, they had to release McLemore when his so-called sprained wrist healed miraculously overnight because those ignorant military doctors were examining *his* wrist, not McLemore's.

So they kind of looked alike, were tall and built somewhat the same, even bore a slight facial resemblance-- and had the same first three letters in their last names-- but couldn't the idiots see that McLemore was a gutless candy. Not only gutless but too stupid to keep up the pose and fake the bum ankle well enough that they would keep his yellow ass in there and not send him out to face ground fire before the counterfeit Lance Corporal Reese McLemore would.

Then to get taken out by friendly fire on his first day out, the real McLemore really screwed things up royal. It forced *him* to maintain the bogus identity, not only for the short duration of the ground offensive, but after-- or face court martial, even imprisonment for impersonating another Marine. Hell, McLachin swore, McLemore was no Marine, not that bastard who had screwed his life over like he had.

He could see Breezy's face when she got the wire notifying her that her husband, Zachary (Zed) McLachin, had been killed in action. He could also

UNDER FRIENDLY FIRE

remember those long confused, desperate months of ducking visits from McLemore's family upon his return to the States, and those stupid-ass typewritten letters to them to cover up the truth.

Not a day had gone by when he did not want to telephone Breezy and tell *her* the truth. He would have called her every day if they had not seemed to suspect something, those weasly military investigators, the moment he stepped off the plane. They would have bugged his phone and her phone in a minute and been throwing his ass in the stinking stockade after putting him through the third degree in some kangaroo court.

Then what would he tell his old man? That he wasn't a blasted war hero at all but a busted Marine? Not only busted but booted out, a McLachin booted out of the United States Marines.

Then yesterday when it all unravelled, when McLemore's brother paid an unscheduled visit to the base and the whole gig was up and they started carting him in front of one empty-suited officer after another in a drowning sea of red tape before assigning that dumb non-com to drive him to the stockade...

That was the only part he regretted. The guy was okay, just doing his job; he had even taken the cuffs off him on the way there in the unmarked car. But dammit, he should have known better than to try and take away Zed McLachin's freedom, to deprive him of his given right to say to hell with all of you, I'm out of here, the whole nine yards and that's that.

Zed McLachin could still hear the guy's neck snap. He had barely touched him and next thing he was doing was laying his still hulk on the grass and driving off with his car, the one he abandoned in Kansas City for the hot-wired Mustang he drove to Dexter non-stop in the damn non-stop rain.

It was close to midnight when he got out, ran up to Breezy's door. *Their* door. Where the hell was she? And that note from that old black woman she used to run to when they had an argument or when she didn't want to give him none-- what was he to make of that?

Did she think it was any all-fired fun to run through that damn rain and go see that ancient nigger-bitch? Did she think it was any fun to slit her wrinkled black throat when she wouldn't tell me where my own wife was?

Or to run back and start combing that lousy, no-count town without being spotted by someone who would call the stinking law, to drive to The Hopper, wait in the damned parking lot for a lousy hour before it emptied out completely to see if you were in there...or to end up busting into Pop Daniels' place like I never seen it before and find that snapshot over the bar with old Pop and Holt-- and you and some sonofabitch I never set eyes on making cozy with *my* whore-wife?

Chapter 29

Fire

UNDER FRIENDLY FIRE

TWENTY-NINE

Jimmy Riskin watched a piece of his dream rise up in angry flames. Not even the relentless rain could check the fire and belching smoke. *Pop Daniels' Dugout and Sports Bar* was dying as swiftly as it was born and, with it, his and Breezy's small stakes, and Pop and Holt's bigger ones, were dying with it. Holt had called him, stirred him from his sleep to tell him. Now he and Holt and Pop himself kept the fire vigil as Dexter's overmatched hook and ladder volunteers fought vainly to contain the rampaging holocaust.

"Glad you dogged me about that policy, Holt," Daniels was saying through the pain, determinedly trying to hide the tears that had welled up in *both* his eyes, his good and his bad one. It was the only thing the rain was any good for.

"Reachable dreams," Riskin muttered under his breath, not trying to hide a thing.

"What was that?" Holt asked distractedly.

MICHAEL CORNELL

"They're just no good unless they're reachable," Riskin answered anyway. He did not know whether Holt heard him or not. It did not seem to matter.

First the betting cards. Then the impromptu visit from the black leather jackets on their Harleys. Now the fire obliterating everything. Riskin turned, walked back to his Jeep, left the others to witness the cremation.

In less than a quarter of an hour, he was pushing past the black maid in her red woolen robe, through the foyer and into the study. They were both standing there. Rance Fallon in the middle of the room, Whitney Fallon in the corner by the ceiling-high bookcase with first editions that had never been opened. They were dressed as though it were time for afternoon cocktails and not something-past-three in the morning. But it was the way they were standing and the distance between them that stopped him.

"Riskin," Fallon said before he could open fire, even if he had wanted to, "I know all about it and I am sincerely sorry."

The most astonishing thing about it, Riskin thought, was that it actually *sounded* sincere and not like the predictable condolences of someone who was acting-- and Fallon *was* an actor.

"I know what you must be thinking," he continued in the same intonation, "but I swear I had nothing to do with it." He added: "and neither did

UNDER FRIENDLY FIRE

any of my people as far as I can tell. Deputy Clemens called me and I was as shocked as anybody. I even asked if I could come out and help our volunteer fire fighters put it out. He told me it was too late for anybody to do anything."

Riskin had been there a whole minute and he still had not uttered a word. He could not. There was something in Fallon's manner, something in his voice that prevented him. When Fallon spoke again, he knew what it was:

"Seems like a bad night all around," he suddenly intimated and Riskin knew he was not talking about the fire *or* the rain. "Seems my dear wife Whitney has informed me that she's leaving me."

Riskin looked at Whitney Fallon. She was not looking at either of them.

The large skinhead in uniform, Dexter law, burst into the room.

"Mayor, your honor," he nearly coughed, his breath all but dissipated, "more trouble: the old black woman Ginny Walker's done had her throat slashed. Breezy McLachin found her in her shack in a pool of blood!"

Fallon looked across at Riskin. "Looks like your firestarter, whoever he is, had other things on his mind besides burning down sports bars."

MICHAEL CORNELL

Riskin did not wait for particulars. All he could think about was Breezy. He bolted out of the house as fast as he could run.

The reachable was fast falling out of reach. He could feel it in the night, in the fire, in his gut.

Chapter 30

Return

UNDER FRIENDLY FIRE

THIRTY

She hoped at first it was the rain slamming against her front door. Or the bulky law returning to ask her more questions. She knew it was neither.

From her bedroom, lying there still shivering in her soaking-wet work uniform, she was staring at the shadowy form looming in her doorway for the first time in twelve months.

The tall, square-built frame said it was *him*. The glazed eyes catching an unseen light source said it was somebody else. The reflecting gaze spoke of an animal totally alien to her, the way her father would describe a rabid dog to her as a small girl.

For a flashing moment she became absolutely certain that this was *not* Zed McLachin.

"Breezy," he said in a low voice that told her otherwise, an almost-animal sound that held the frenzy of the wind and the rain that was now gusting through the open front door.

She could not say his name.

He lunged forward, leaped heavily on top of her and began clawing at the thin covering of her uniform.

"Breezy," he called out again in the darkness.

She could not answer, could not even scream.

He ripped away her panties, forced his loins against hers.

She felt the pressure of his superior weight enveloping her, nothing else.

"Breezy!" he cried out again, louder against the howling wind.

The animal was too enraged to be aroused. She felt nothing but limpness. The smothering mass collapsed, beaten by its own angryness, its own unfocused fury.

Now it was being torn away from her. Somebody had wrested it away, was grappling violently on the floor with its long sinuous massiveness. Momentarily, Breezy McLachin was staring down at her past and her future.

The larger hands of the one were choking the throat of the other whose own hands were gripping the throat of the larger one, her attacker, Ginny Walker's murderer.

With a solitary flash of the military handgun that Zed McLachin had given her for her own personal protection, Breezy McLachin blew away her past forever.

UNDER FRIENDLY FIRE

With the small explosion the roar of the wind seemed to subside ever so slightly. Maybe Jimmy Riskin imagined it. And now, as he held her trembling in his arms, the words of the song came back:
"They never stood in the dark with you, love..."
He could not remember how the rest of the verse went.
It would come.